I0691418

"Yes, Cops Do It, – Oh Yeah!"

First Edition

Published by The Nazca Plains Corporation
Las Vegas, Nevada
2009

ISBN: 978-1-935509-38-7

Published by

The Nazca Plains Corporation ®
4640 Paradise Rd, Suite 141
Las Vegas NV 89109-8000

PUBLISHER'S NOTE
"Yes, Cops Do It, – Oh Yeah!" is a work of fiction created wholly
by *Wade Wright's* imagination. All characters are fictional and any
resemblance to any persons living or deceased is purely by accident.
No portion of this book reflects any real person or events.

Cover Photos, Les Byerley and Dmitriy Eremenkov
Art Director, Blake Stephens

DEDICATION

To every law enforcement officer that serves our public with the dignity, and the skill that they each represent. To each, we say "Thank you!"

"YES, COPS DO IT, – OH YEAH!"

First Edition

Wade Wright

CONTENTS

TWO BROTHERS AND TWO OFFICERS

BRAD'S EARLY MORNING WALK HOME

ONE HOT COP, OFFICER GREG

TWO BROTHERS AND TWO OFFICERS

A Boner Book

CHAPTER ONE:

The Speeding Ticket

"Oh shit!! Jimmy exclaimed, to his brother Tom, as the State Patrol Officer turned on his overheads and pulled Jimmy over. "God Tom! I wasn't speeding was I? I didn't do anything wrong, did I?"

Officer Jackson got out of his patrol car and as he approached the driver's side of Jimmy's car, he asked, "Do you have any idea, at all, of how fast you were driving back there?"

Jimmy replied that he obviously did not, since he thought he was within the speed limit, but since he was getting pulled over, he had to assume that he must have been driving faster than he thought.

Officer Jackson asked for Jimmy's driver's license and after retrieving it, he turned to go back to his patrol car to do a computer check of the license. Jimmy looked into his door's rear view mirror as Officer Jackson started to leave, and rather excitedly turned to Tom and asked, "Oh my God Tom! Did you see the ass on that guy? Shit man did you see the tight ass on him? God man, oh shit! Those damn uniform pants kiss his ass like, oh shit, just like—oh man, —oh shit, they are hot!"

Tom rather faintly said, "Uh, Jim, uh, —Jim, turn to your left!"

Jim turned to look to his left and very surprisingly discovered that Officer Jackson was standing right beside his open window. He had heard Jim's entire statement. Officer Jackson had returned back to Jimmy's car to inquire about the license being expired, as opposed to continuing on to his patrol car as Jimmy had thought he had done.

Officer Jackson bent down, placed his hands on the lower edge of the window and asked, "Driving through from Ohio, I assume?"

Jimmy very cautiously and very shyly, replied, "Yes, —yes sir!"

"Seems as though we might have a slight problem here, young man. This license expired more than six months ago. Driving the speed that you were driving, and driving on a very expired license, especially one from out of state, and one that is more than two months expired, does give me the reason to remove you from that car, place you in the back seat of my patrol car, and take you in. Do you understand your position here, young man?"

Jimmy and Tom both found it rather interesting that the officer kept referring to Jimmy as "young man" since it really did not appear to either one of them that Jimmy was hardly any younger than the officer was, himself.

Jimmy was 24, stood about 5'8", weighted in at about 170 pounds, of pretty solid, sports activity muscle. Tom was two years younger, aged 22, stood right at six feet tall, and since he too was a very active athlete, he carried a nicely packaged 190 pounds of rock solid, man muscle.

Officer Jackson appeared to Jimmy and Tom as being perhaps only 24 or 25 years old himself, and once they did get a chance to discuss it completely, they did both agree that Officer Jackson was one hot looking patrolman with his uniform fitting every muscle and every curve of, what they guessed, was about 220 pounds of tight and very solid muscle, nicely attached to a very strong looking structure of about six foot one or two. Massive chest and one hell of a hot and very firm ass. Of course, that was the attribute that Jimmy had brought to Tom's attention, although it was done at a rather inappropriate time.

Jimmy replied in the affirmative to Officer Jackson's question to, —if he did understand the circumstances or not. After Jimmy replied, Officer Jackson told him to sit tight, and he returned to his patrol car.

As Officer Jackson sat in his patrol car, obviously reading his computer screen, Jim and Tom discussed the "just what was going on here" situation. Tom pointed out to Jim that he had tried, in vain, to get him to shut up about the officer's ass when he saw the officer returning to the side of the car, but that Jimmy just kept up the, "almost screaming," about how hot it was. They slightly discussed the whole package that Officer Jackson presented to the visual, and they of course individually wondered, and did share it with each other, that since Officer Jackson was a black man, did he have as much packaged in front of those uniform pants as they had always been led to believe black men packed.

"Tom, I have never heard anything about some two month thing on an expired license, have you? What in the hell was he talking about?"

"Jim, I have no idea either. I have never heard of anything like that. All I know is that since he had just heard you almost telling him, how you wanted to kiss his ass, I didn't think it would be too smart to ask what he was talking about. Right now, I think maybe we had just better let it go. We could get him real pissed, especially since he heard you kind of loving his ass, so I think we had just better let it go. He's not making any remarks about your stupid statements, so don't push it, man!"

After quite some time in the patrol car, Officer Jackson re-approached the side of Jimmy's car, leaned down on the widow ledge again and stated, "Okay guys! We have some talking to do here."

Jimmy looked at the officer's face and then with no self control, looked down at Officer Jackson's crotch. The, slightly previous, discussion with brother Tom about wondering if the officer was well packed, became just too much for him to maintain control over. He did not intend to look down, he had simply lost control of himself.

Officer Jackson saw Jimmy glance down.

"Out of the car, please." Officer Jackson addressed to Jimmy.

"Step over here beside my patrol car, and place your hands on the roof. I need to do a pat down." Then looking at Tom, he said, "You stay there! Do not get out of the car!"

Officer Jackson then took Jimmy by the arm and led him to the field side of the patrol car, out of the light of the head lights and once again told Jimmy to place his hands on the roof of the car. Jimmy thought it was rather different, well from all of the TV police shows that he had seen, that the officer had him at the side of the patrol car, on the rather darker side, away from the highway area, and not at the trunk of his own car, where the headlights lit up the area.

Jimmy placed his hands on the roof of the car, and Officer Jackson then reached down, grabbed ahold of Jimmy's left ankle and pulled it to the side. This, of course, slightly shook Jimmy off of balance and he had to rather quickly re-adjust his stance so that he did not fall. Officer Jackson then did the same thing to the right ankle and once again Jimmy almost fell over. Officer Jackson then started a very detailed body pat. Slowly and very deliberately, he body searched Jimmy. Tom was in the position to where he could watch from his side door rear view mirror and watch as closely as possible, to the actions that were taking place back beside the patrol car. Since Jimmy and the officer were on the darker side of the car, it was rather hard to see everything, but Tom certainly did question all of the "whats and whys" of what was happening. He questioned just why Jimmy was being body searched, and he also questioned why the officer was being so deliberate and so slow in doing it.

As Officer Jackson continued his careful pat down of Jim, Jim did suddenly realize that an additional patrol car was now pulling in behind Officer Jackson's patrol car. The second patrol car stopped, an officer got out of the car and Officer Jackson then told him, "The other one is in the passenger seat."

The second patrolman approached the passenger side of the car, opened the door and instructed Tom to get out, go back to the side of the patrol car, and present yourself to be searched.

Tom did as he was instructed, knowing that he was to put his hands on the roof of the car and to spread his feet in preparation to being body searched, but he certainly did feel that the wording, "present yourself to be searched", was very unusual language to be used.

As Tom and the additional officer approached the position where Jimmy and Officer Jackson were positioned, Officer Jackson then said, "Officer Tyler, you take over on this one, and I'll start on that one."

Officer Tyler could almost be considered an identical twin to Officer Jackson, except, —he was a white man. Same, damn hot muscular structure, right at the same age, and carrying just as hot of an ass in his State Highway Patrolman uniform pants, as Officer Jackson's ass was in his.

Both Tom and Jimmy were completely confused as to what in the hell was going on. Officer Tyler re-started a complete body pat of Jim, and Officer Jackson then started his very slow and deliberate body search of Tom.

Both Jimmy and Tom realized that their respective body searches and body pats were turning out to be a little more than just "normal." Of all of the TV police programs that they had watched over the years, never had they ever seen a patrolman do as much crotch rubbing and grabbing as they were each getting. Jimmy did not mind, it was actually turning him on, —kind of, but Tom was not feeling too comfortable with this activity. To Jimmy, it was feeling good, even though he had absolutely no idea of why it was all happening. As he felt the big strong officer's hands rub up and down along his body and up under his arm pits, as well as up between his legs, he threw his head up, closed his eyes and simply enjoyed it. Even if, it was something, that was not supposed to be a good experience. He decided that if he was in deep trouble, he was at least going to enjoy the sick little part of getting rubbed, groped and felt up by one hell of a hot looking cop.

As the searching slowly continued, and with great detail of inspection happening from both officers, Officer Jackson turned toward Officer Tyler and said, "Officer Tyler, as I told you on the phone, these two are a little different than the others. I haven't told them just yet of how they can avoid that ticket, but since that one, the one you are now taking care of, was all hot and excited about seeing my ass, I kind of think these two just might be a little more anxious and cooperative than our past guys have been."

To Jimmy and Tom, that statement was a complete shock and the meaning behind it, a total mystery.

"Great!" Officer Tyler replied. "It's about time we finally find ourselves some cooperative men!"

Jimmy tried to turn and ask just what they were referring to, when Officer Tyler spoke up and told him, "Hey, man! You were not given permission to speak, so just stand there and be quiet!" And with that instruction, Officer Tyler then reached around to the front of Jim and with each hand, squeezed each of Jim's tits. "Like that? That feel good?" He inquired of Jim.

Jim, really did, want to kind of let out a very vigorous "Yes, God yes! That feels good!" yell, but managed to refrain from showing any anxiety, due to his complete confusion as to just what was happening here. Jimmy simply kind of shook his head yes, as if to attempt to show some respect back to the officer and to attempt an agreeable position, so as to not piss the officer off any.

Officer Jackson then reached around to the front of Tom, grabbed ahold of his left tit through his T-shirt, and at the same time grabbed ahold of his crotch. "Officer Tyler, this one is going to be a good one. You haven't felt the dick on this one yet have you?"

"No, no I sure haven't. You took him away from me as soon as I got him out of the car. Feels good to you, does it?"

"Oh hell yes! And you want to know something? He may be trying to act a little scared and timid, but for some funny reason, his dick is not cooperating with that. The more I squeeze it, the bigger it gets."

"Hmmmmm!" Officer Tyler expressed. Maybe, just maybe, we have finally hit the ole jack pot here Officer Jackson! Maybe you have finally stopped the right car!"

"Officer, uhh, officer!" Jim attempted to say, but was once again firmly told, "Shut up! You have not been given permission to speak. Stand there and shut the hell up!"

7

Jim and Tom were not comfortable with the actions or the attitudes. Both men were definitely on the side of concern about their safety, although Jim was now admitting to himself that this type of forced action was kind of a turn on to him. He knew that his most private thoughts and fantasies included some actions similar to this, but he had always thought of them in a much more controlled environment, not out along the side of a highway, late at night, with no way of screaming for help if he felt like he needed it.

Jim knew that Tom was somewhat active in the gay world, not nearly as active as he personally was, but he sure did not know if this type of action was scaring the hell out of him, or was he managing to find some rather weird fun in it, as he was. Part of his excitement was all of the strange and weird unknowns that were showing up all of a sudden.

He knew for certain, now anyway, that he had not been driving above the speed limit, and there really was no valid reason to get pulled over. His driver's license could not be expired! They are issued for five years, and he re-newed his when he turned 21, and that was only three years ago. And, as he and Tom had discussed, neither one of them had ever heard anything that relates to a two months thing on an expired license. Officer Jackson had not given him the license back, nor let him see it after he said it was expired. This searching was not exactly a searching, it was really turning out to be more of groping session, with some legality backing it up. Neither officer had grabbed ahold of his dick yet, but Officer Jackson had already exclaimed how nice Tom's dick was feeling, and had made remarks about it getting harder when he grabbed ahold of it. The referred to phone call to the other officer? Not the state highway radio system? They called each other on their cell phones? All of the talk about how this time they finally hit the jack pot? What in the hell was happening here? This was not a normal traffic stop. Are these guys even real cops? The actions were getting Jim rather sexually excited, but all of the "funny stuff", was getting him very concerned and quite confused. He wanted the "funny stuff" to just magically go away so that he could concentrate on the more exciting aspects of this, "highway road stop."

Jim looked over at Tom, and Tom attempted an expression of confusion as to just what in the hell was happening here. Tom knew not to talk or attempt to ask any questions. He had heard Jim get shut up earlier, and he did not wish to make either of the patrolmen mad at him. He knew he was in a situation where obeying was the only thing to do. He knew that if one of the officers spoke, gave instructions and orders, that he would simply have to do as ordered, with no back-talk.

Both officers continued their very extensive body searching and what had now turned into, —plain out and out, groping. Officer Tyler grabbed ahold of Jim's crotch and exclaimed, "Shit man! You thought that boy's toy was good, shit man, reach over here and feel this one. Officer Jackson, I think we have ourselves some serious meat toys here! This one likes it. You like it, don't you boy?"

Jim was in total confusion as to how he thought he should answer that question. Once again he wanted to scream "Yes," but at the same time he refrained himself since he just did not know if he could find this as fun, which was what he wanted to do, or was he and his brother in some real danger with some really dangerous type of guys? The mixture of possible bodily danger, the complete confusion, and his real internal desires to be able to enjoy this type of outrageous sexual actions were absolutely and totally confusing Jim. He wanted so badly to really be able to enjoy this total submission to two hot and hunky cops, but at the same time, he really did not know if they were just being playful or on the verge of being very, very dangerous to a couple of gay guys. Had his stupid mistake, of commenting on Officer Jackson's hot looking ass, really gotten them in some very dangerous stuff?

Officer Jackson reached over as suggested by his co-officer, grabbed ahold of Jim's dick and immediately grabbed a bigger, and a much more forceful, handful. He grabbed it and then he forcefully squeezed it!

"Drop his pants! Drop his pants! I want to see that thing! Drop his pants and get that thing out!"

Suddenly without any further warning, Officer Tyler turned Jim completely around, unbuckled his belt, unbuttoned Jim's 501's, pulled them down, and then said, "Oh shit man! Look at that bulge in those briefs!"

With his 501's now on his shoe tops, Jim stood there with a rock hard cock sticking out as far as possible, being confined only slightly with the weak fabric of his BVD's.

Tom turned toward Jimmy and saw his ragging hard-on sticking out. Officer Jackson let loose of Tom's shoulder and reached over and slid his hand down into the front of Jim's briefs. When the officer's hand reached the tip of Jimmy's dick that made it stiffen, even harder. Officer Jackson grabbed ahold of it, pulled it forward and forced it to emerge out of the top of Jimmy's briefs.

"Oh shit! Oh shit! Officer Tyler that is one hot dick! That is going to taste so damn good!"

That had been the first really comfortable comment that either Jim or Tom had heard, ever since they had been stopped. If that officer can make a comment about a dick tasting good, then maybe everything would be okay and they would not be trashed and left for dead beside the highway.

Seeing the hard-on that Jimmy had, made Tom get more excited. Although he and Jimmy talked a lot of sex, they had never been the type of brothers that showed "their stuff" to each other, or had sex when the other guy was around. Tom actually did not know that his brother supported such a healthy cock. He had not seen it hard since back in high school days. Of all of the talk that they had shared about black men and the supposed size of their cocks, never did Tom realize that his own brother could stand his own if, comparing it with a black man's. The size of it, even though it was on his own brother, got Tom all excited.

Since Officer Jackson still had one hand on Tom's crotch, he immediately realized the reaction that Tom had when he looked at Jim's now exposed stick of meat. Officer Jackson looked back at Tom, grinned, then looked down at Tom's crotch and simply said, "It feels confined, don't it? You like seeing your buddy's big boner, don't you? I'm sure you have used that one a lot though, haven't you? Still gets you all excited though, uh?"

"He's my brother!" Tom simply said without much emphasis.

"Oh! Oh, so that's the story here, uh? Two brothers! So maybe we have a couple of guys here Officer Tyler that don't do each other. Is that right, man? They check out officer's asses together, but they don't use each other? Right?"

Tom did not reply. Now the confusion had really set in on him. He was excited! He was hard! He was hoping that all of this was some kind of a wild sex session starting to happen, but at the same time, —these were officers of the law,—they were standing out beside a highway, with traffic passing by, and with Jim's pants down and his hard-on dick standing out, and besides, he and his brother never do sex stuff when the other guy is around. He was completely surprised that this officer, the hunk of a muscle black man himself, would get so excited about the dick on Jim. After all, he was the type of a man that everybody always wants to get the pants off of, if for no other reason, than to just see if he is hung with one of the big, long, thick, meaty, black, sticks that everybody talks about being on black men.

Officer Jackson then looked at Officer Tyler and said, "I'm getting way too anxious and turned on here! Let's put one of them in the back seat of my car, let the other one follow you in his car so that it's not left out here on the highway, and let's get to the playroom over in the barn. I want to get to that one. I want him on the table. Let's get going."

Then turning to Jim, Officer Jackson then told him, "It's either cooperate, —go with Officer Tyler and myself, enjoy some good time together in a nice little ole country barn playroom, equipped with all kind of nice shinny, fun, equipment, or have me turn in your traffic ticket, which I'm kind of sure you don't really want me to do, since —oh as I kind of remember it, —two, of us, me and Officer Tyler here, had to chase you for about, —oh 25 or 30 miles, at speeds up to —oh probably 100 miles an hour, before we could finally get you to stop. Officer, Tyler, is that about the way you remember it?"

"Yep, sure sounds pretty close to me! Yeah—that's what happened. Yeah, —I sure can remember that real well now that you kind of remind me of what happened! Yep, that's what I remember!"

Officer Jackson then looked at Jim and asked, "Well man! Your choice is, go with us, let us take you to our quiet little playroom in the barn, let us find out how much you two like some of the fun stuff we have there, or as I already said, let me turn in your traffic ticket, and then just let the boys down at the ole jail house use you any ole way they can find fit to use you, since you will be there for quite some time, —especially since Officer Tyler and I had such a hard time getting you pulled over. And I'm sure you already know how a bunch of guys, all stuck together in a small jail cell, like to find good fun things to do, to new guys once the lights get turned off for the night. You know, a lot of the time, they will kind of stick together and help each other out, when one of them feels like it is time for him to do some exploring in some new guy's ass. You know, when a guy is in there with that bunch, —saying "no," is not a very smart thing to do. The more he yells "no", more guys keep moving in to take advantage of him, and his ass, once they get him held down. Which you want? The playroom, or would you rather be the "play toys" for some jail, full of guys that just might be a hell of a lot more horny than we are, and probably could not care less about how they use some good hot meat like you two?"

Jim and Tom looked at each other, and neither expressed any facial expressions that indicated that they felt like they had any choice in the matter. They both knew that going to the barn was definitely the better of the two choices. Individually, but without letting the other brother know, they each rather liked the idea of being forced to have sex like this, having no say or control at all, doing it with a couple of hot muscle cops, in a barn playroom, hidden away someplace, and finally being forced to actually have gay sex, in front of his brother, with his brother in the room, or maybe even involved with the, —what is then happening. Tom had always wanted to play with Jim, but he had never had the nerve to tell him so. Tonight might be a night that he had been hoping for.

The idea of the "playroom" and the comments about the "equipment" that was there, was a little scary. Neither Tom nor Jim, had ever spent any time in a man's "playroom" before. They did not know what to expect, especially in regards to the term, equipment. All of their sex activities, had been pretty tame. This did not sound so tame! But the idea of being thrown into a jail, full of probably dirty, drunk, and horny guys that could care less if it's a man or a woman, or what body part he was using, was a definite no, no! All for fun, yes! All for danger, no! Learning something new, at the hands of two hunks, especially ones built like these two patrolmen, a definite yes! Jim and Tom both realized that maybe their days of not doing sex in front of the other guy, just might be over. But then, both of the brothers also realized, that to finally be a little more open with each other, just might be a step in the right direction. It was a direction that Tom had been hoping for.

Jim told Officer Jackson and Officer Tyler, "We're with you. We'll do as you say!"

Both Jim and Tom, each, did realize that they were now opening the door to some completely new experiences, and could possibly be walking through the door of opportunity, of enjoying some good gay sex, with not only the hot and hunky, —built like God cops, —but perhaps, maybe, with each other too!

Secretly, and especially Tom, they were each looking forward to this new sexual adventure of maybe having the chance to explore the body of his own brother. Now that Tom knew that his brother was supporting such a nice healthy piece of meat, he was feeling real anxious to get to the barn, wherever the cops were talking about, so he could see if maybe he could explore Jim's own personal piece of equipment, in addition to the equipment that the officers had there in the playroom. Tom was getting really anxious to get the show on the road. The idea of being played with by the two cops, in their playroom, wherever that might be, in addition to being forced, by them, to play with his own brother, was getting him really all hot and bothered. He had, had dreams like this before, but for it to be happening in real life, was way more than he ever expected!

CHAPTER TWO:

Your Ass is Mine, Boy

Officer Jackson put Tom in the back seat of his cruiser, and told Jim to follow Officer Tyler to the State Highway Department, so that they could drop off the cruisers for servicing, and not have the two cruisers sitting at the farm.

Officer Jackson told Tom, "We're gonna drop off the cruisers at the department since it's only about five minutes out of the way, and since Officer Tyler and I both have the next two days off, we can get our cars all serviced and taken care of. Besides, I really don't want two Highway Patrol cruisers sitting around at the farm for two days. When we get to the department, you and I'll use my personal car, and Officer Tyler and your big brother can follow us in your car. You riding okay back there?"

Tom replied that yes he was, and then asked, "Uhh, sir! What is going to go on when we get to the barn? I've never been in some guy's playroom before. Sir, I'm not sure I will know what you expect me to do."

"Hey boy!" Officer Jackson replied. "Don't get all scared about what we are going to do. Officer Tyler and I just like to get some new meat once in awhile, and when I saw you two guys drive past my hiding area, I decided that two guys, from out of state, looked like a great deal to me. So, anyway,

13

that's why you guys got stopped. Of course, finding out that you both like cop's asses, that was a complete surprise. I mean, you like male butts too, don't you? I know your brother does. He almost told me to my face! Before we even got you guys out of the car, he was kind of telling me that he wanted to plant his face right up between my butt cheeks. You play with guys too? Like your brother?"

"Uhh, yeah." Tom rather shyly answered. "Yeah, I'm gay too, but Jim's got a lot more experience, than I do. He's had gay friends around him for years, and I was always the little brother that was kind of pushed aside, so I haven't done some of the stuff that Jim has. Officer, I really don't know if I'm going to be able to do stuff like you and the other officer expect. I've only played with a few guys. Really, I guess I need to let you know that I don't know how to do a lot of stuff that I know guys do together."

"Hey, Tom, —right? Your name is Tom, right?"

"Yeah, it's Tom. Yeah that's right!"

"Okay Tom, don't get yourself all scared. I appreciate you telling me that you think you are kind of inexperienced. I'll make sure we remember that when we get to the barn. Okay? You and your brother have played with each other of course, I assume. Right?"

"Oh Sir, you're kind of embarrassing me. No, we never have. No, I've never played with him, and I have to admit that not until you took his dick out of his pants tonight, had I ever seen him have a hard-on. Well, maybe when I was in junior high and he was in high school, but never since then. Sir, I really did not know Jim had such a big dick until you pulled it out tonight. Sir, I do admit I'm kind of jealous of it. Mine's not that big."

"Well, Tom. Are you wanting to play with his dick or not? You want it now that you've seen how big it is?"

"Yeah, yeah I know I do. I've wanted to play with him for a long time now, but then I didn't know it was so fucking big. Now that I've seen it, I wish we had been playing with it for a long time, but since I was the little brother, I never felt like I could tell him I wanted to see it or suck on it. Do you think maybe I'll get to tonight? Or are you guys going to do stuff to us that doesn't let me get ahold of him?"

"No, Tom, no! We're not going to be doing anything that would keep you two apart. All four of us will be in one playroom, and I'm sure everybody will get a chance to do whatever, and with whomever, he wants. Tell you what! I'll remember that you do want to use your brother, and I'll make sure we play stuff so that happens. Okay? Is that Okay with you?"

"Oh yes Sir! Oh yes! Yes, I really would like that if you would help me do that. Sir, I'd really like that a lot!"

"Hey Tom, here's the highway department. Now if I just let you get out of this car nice and quietly, so that nobody notices us, you won't give me any trouble will you? I'll pull up beside my car, and you just get out of here and get in my car and everything will be okay! Right? Tom, listen, don't try anything funny! I've still got that traffic stop ticket, and if I need to use it to protect myself and Officer Tyler, I will. Understand?"

"Yeah, oh yes, —I do understand. Sir, I want to get to that barn as badly as you do now, especially since you have told me that you will make sure I get a chance to do some stuff with Jimmy, so no sir, I will not give you any problem. I promise! I promise!"

"Good boy! Good boy!" Officer Jackson said.

"Here. My car is the gray Buick. The doors are unlocked. You quietly get out of here, and go get in my car. Don't you run! I've got that ticket that I can use! Remember?"

"Oh yes Sir, I do remember. Sir, I guess you don't quite understand how anxious I am to get a chance to play with you and the other officer. Sir, you are a big strong black man, and I've never had a chance to play with a guy anything like you, so Sir, I will not be giving you any kind of trouble. I'm too anxious for you and me to do some stuff together. I wanna see all of you naked and bare. I really wanna see your dick and your butt!"

Then with a big grin on his face, Tom added, "I'm anxious except for maybe the fact that my ass has never had anything up in it like I'm sure the size of your cock is, so I may not be able to take you if you're planning on fucking my ass! You planning on fucking my ass, Sir? Are you?"

Officer Jackson realized that Tom was actually getting anxious to get to the barn, and as he laughed back, he reached over the seat back, rubbed Tom's head, and said, "Hey boy. Get out of here and get in my car. It will take me only about two minutes to turn my cruiser in, and then I'll be right back."

Tom opened the door, got out, and Officer Jackson then drove his patrol cruiser over into a different parking spot. Officer Jackson got out of his cruiser, looked over toward Tom and realized that Tom was leaning against the side of his Buick, watching him from across the parking lot.

Officer Tyler and Jim had already gotten to the highway headquarters, and Officer Tyler was standing outside of Jim's car waiting to talk to him.

"How's it going with the kid?" Officer Tyler asked.

"Not bad! Not bad at all! How you and the other one doing? Think he is okay?"

"Well, since we were in separate cars, I've only had about a minute to talk to him once we got here, but he sounds real scared. He said something about how he would have made a run for it if Tommy had not been in your car. I'll find out more while we go on to the barn. I'll fill you in once we get there, Okay?"

"Yeah Okay!" Officer Jackson replied. "Talk to you then."

Officer Jackson returned to his car, and to his complete surprise discovered that Tom had taken the front seat instead of the back seat, as he had normally expected.

As he got in the car, Officer Jackson said, "Well boy! This is a complete surprise. I figured you would want to stay as far away from me as you could, for as long as you could! I just naturally figured you'd be in the back seat. What do we owe this change of events to?"

Tom looked at the officer and said, "We owe this change of events to the fact that I have never had the chance to play with a guy anything like you, and if we are going to be on back roads until we get to the barn, then I want to do something that I never thought I'd ever do, and that is play with you while you drive. I've read stories about guys that suck on some guy while they are on the road, and that has always gotten me all excited, but I sure never thought I would get to be one of those guys. Can I pull your dick out and lick it while we drive?"

"Tom my boy, you are getting to be a complete surprise to me. I thought for sure that of the two of you, you would be the one that we might have some trouble with, but shit man, you are a real go getter, aren't you? You really want to get it on, don't you?"

"Yeah, yes I do! I have felt for years now that Jimmy was always the one that got to have all of the fun, and Sir, should I call you Sir, tonight I want to be the one that really has the fun!"

"Yeah, Tom, —yes! Do call me Sir. Don't do that because I'm a highway patrolman, though, but do that because tonight I am going to be your "Daddy." You understand what I mean when I tell you that I am going to be your Daddy?"

"Yes Sir, yes I do Sir! That much I do understand Sir! May I service you Sir?"

Officer Jackson immediately unbuckled his uniform belt, unbuttoned his uniform pants, unzipped the pants, reached in his briefs, pulled out one gorgeous ten inch, thick, black, hard, and stiff dick, —looked at Tom and said, "Yes boy! Yes you may service me! Yes boy, that sausage is now yours! It will take us about 20 minutes to get to the barn, and I want to feel your mouth on that stick that entire 20 minutes. Do you have any questions before you slam your sweet little mouth down on that stick? Cause, once you do, I want you to stay on it till we get to the barn. Understand?"

"Oh yes Sir! Yes, I understand! I have no questions Sir!"

Tom grabbed ahold of Officer Jackson's stick, slowly licked the tip of it, opened his mouth wide and proceeded to take as much as possible of the entire ten inch length down his throat. He choked and coughed a few times, and Officer Jackson knew that Tom was experiencing something bigger than he had ever done before. As Tom attempted to do the best that he could, Officer Jackson slid his car seat back just a little so that Tom would have a little more room between the officer's stomach and the steering wheel. Officer Jackson softly rubbed Tom's head as Tom continued to try and get all of the big brown stick down in his throat.

"Eat me boy! Eat me!" Officer Jackson encouraged Tom.

As they turned onto another country road, Officer Jackson told Tom, "Hey boy. We are just about ready to turn into the farm drive. Why don't you sit up and kind of help me get all put back together before we get to the barn. Let's kind of try and keep it our little secret that you've been practicing on me. I just kind of like the fact that you and I have already had a slight chance to get some stuff started, and I'd kind of like to keep it that way. Is that okay with you?"

"Yes, oh yes!" Tom replied. "Yeah, I'd like that! That kind of makes me feel a little closer to you. Yeah, I'd like that!"

As they parked both cars, everybody got out and went into the barn. Officer Jackson then unlocked and opened an inside door. He hit a light switch and Jim and Tom both let out an, "Oh, my God!"

The inner room was about 20 by 30 feet in size, had a black leather sling hanging in one corner, a padded table with chains and straps on each end, a queen size mattress in one side of the room, some chains hanging in different places around the room, and on the opposite side of the room, a large counter with a number of shelves above it. What was in the closed door cabinets, Jim and Tom did not know, but on the exposed shelves, they saw a complete assortment of chains, ropes, cans of grease, rubber gloves, dildos, butt plugs and quite a number of items that they simply did not recognize.

Jim and Tom were standing in front of the two officers. Officer Tyler asked, "Well men! Like what you see so far?"

"Oh shit man! Please men, please, I've never been anyplace like this. Men, please I don't think we should be here!" Jim exclaimed.

"Hey cool it man!" Officer Tyler replied. You are safe, —nothing except fun is going to happen to you. Why don't you two nice hunks of Ohio meat get yourselves all undressed and Officer Jackson and I will get ourselves kind of nude too. Put you clothes over there on that bench, boys."

Jim very slowly moved forward toward the bench that Officer Tyler had mentioned. Tom even more slowly moved, but as he did, he turned, looked at Officer Jackson and smiled. Officer Jackson noticed it, and smiled back. He felt that perhaps he and Tom had, in-fact, already created some type of a bonding. He sensed that Tom was not as nervous with this arrangement as his older brother, Jim, was.

Both of the brothers removed all of their clothes, as did the two patrol officers. Jim and Tom placed theirs on the bench, and the officers used individual closets, which they each had available.

"Hey Tyler, why don't you take that Jim guy over to the mattress, and I want to get this Tom guy all tied down on the table for a few minutes."

Jim stood there, completely naked, bare butt out and showing, and his dick completely exposed, but not showing any strength in it.

Tom also stood there completely naked, his bare butt exposed also, but his dick was at attention. Jim noticed. "Shit man! Is this turning you on or something, man?" Jim asked his brother Tom.

"Well, yeah I guess it must be some. Hey guy, I really don't think anything bad is going to happen to us. They come across to me as just a couple of guys that like to have some fun, and they've got a good place to do it in. Really, Jim, I really don't think we are in any trouble! Go for it man, look at the bodies on those guys that we're gonna get to play with! And shit man, I don't know about you, but I sure know I've never had a chance to play with any guy that is as hot as either one of these guys!"

As the two officers heard Tom re-assure his older brother, Officer Tyler entered, "He's right guy. Nothing is going to happen to you guys except for some good guy sex fun, and maybe some things that you've never had a chance to do before. Come on Jim, Officer Jackson wants you and me to get started over here on the mattress. Let's us go over here and we'll do whatever you want to do, to get started. Okay?"

Officer Tyler and Jim went over to the mattress and Tom saw them lay down. He then turned toward Officer Jackson and grinned. Officer Jackson grinned back, and then said, "Your ass is mine boy! Lay down on that table, gut down!"

Tom did as he was instructed, but he was rather surprised at the firm instruction mode that he was given. He had expected Officer Jackson to be much more calm and gentle.

As Tom laid down, Officer Jackson reached down and grabbed ahold of the chain and wrist strap on Tom's left side. He strapped Tom's left wrist into the strap. He then did the right wrist, the left ankle and the right ankle. Tom flipped his head back and forth looking to see just what was happening.

Officer Jackson very gently placed his hands on Tom's back, and slowly started rubbing his back, his neck, shoulders, arms and finally his butt and the crack between each of his butt cheeks. Tom liked the feel of having this big black muscular highway patrolman feeling all of him, and especially knowing that his ass was being used to the enjoyment of the big man. Tom laid there, both arms pulled out and chained down, as were both of his legs, but he was sincerely enjoying this treatment. He was not finding any of it alarming or to his disliking. He was smiling as he felt Officer Jackson slide his hands along his skin. Tom slightly utter, "Yeah, yeah, that feels so good! Touch me, touch me, touch me!"

As Officer Jackson heard Tom utter the encouragements, he climbed up on the leather covered table and straddled Tom's body. Tom attempted to look back, but in his prone, tied and chained down position, he had quite a lot of trouble doing so. For only a very slight moment, he did get a chance to grab one very quick glimpse of the very large, black, thick, stick rod, that he had so gladly managed to chew and suck on earlier, as they drove to the farm. When he had his mouth on it, it did not seem to be so far out of size, but now that it was just above his bare butt, his asshole standing completely exposed, that same dick did look to be almost twice the size that it had earlier. Suddenly Tom had some very major concerns about the fact that he knew his ass was about to be the recipient of it, and he wasn't so sure his ass was going to be able to take it so very easily or very smoothly. He decided that perhaps being completely chained down, totally unable to escape if he so wanted to, perhaps that was the reason that all of a sudden it looked so damn big.

"Oh, Officer Jackson! Officer Jackson, are you planning on fucking me with that thing? Oh shit man, I'm not sure I can take that! That is a lot of dick! Really, I'm not sure I can take that whole thing!"

"Yeah boy, you can take it. You just lay there and relax your ass. I've got a lot of grease on it, and I won't push it in any faster than what I know you can take. Just lay still. My dick and your ass are just about ready to meet each other, and in just about one minute, you are going to be thanking me for giving all of it to you. In just about one minute man, you are gonna find out just what it feels like to have one big black officer's rod resting up in your little asshole."

Officer Jackson positioned himself right above Tom's butt, grabbed ahold of his dick and aimed it for the hole. "Lay still Tom, this big man is about ready to let you know what a big, long, black, thick dick feels like up inside of your ass!"

Slowly Officer Jackson lowered himself and allowed his rod to start its entry into the nice smooth white ass that he had been anxious to get to ever since he first stopped Jim's car. Slowly he lowered and felt the tip of his cock push the edges of Tom's asshole apart, and start its entry. Tom jerked and tried to squirm.

"You're okay! You're okay!" Officer Jackson re-assured Tom. "I know you can feel it, but it's not going to hurt you any. You've shit bigger turds out of that ass than what this dick is. Lay still so I can give all of it to you. You'll like it once it's up in there. You'll be begging for more in just a minute.

Officer Jackson was right. He was very right! Within only a minute or two, he had gotten his entire rod up into Tom's ass and all of a sudden Tom was begging for more. He was pushing his ass, up and back, toward Officer Jackson, as if he was wanting more dick, a lot more dick, rammed up into his ass.

"Yes! Oh gawd yes! Oh shit man that feels so good! Please fuck me hard! Let me feel it. Yeah, —fuck me hard! Please! Please!"

Officer Jackson had gotten the request and the anxiety that he had been waiting for. He had been told to fuck Tom's ass hard, and he did not hesitate to do just that! All of a sudden, all kinds of action were happening on the table. And all of it was Tom getting fucked harder than he had ever been fucked before, and with a dick much larger than any dick he had been fucked with, before, or even seen before!

"Oh shit man! Oh I love it! Fuck me harder! Fuck me! Fuck me! Fuck me!" Tom actually yelled. He knew that his brother Jim had to have heard what he yelled, but right now, and even though he and Jim had never had sex in front of the other guy, he did not care. This action in his butt was way too exciting to try and act timid about it. He was finally getting it good and rough in the ass, and he wasn't about to act like he did not want it. He wanted it, and he wanted it good and rough, and if that was a shock to his big brother, then that is just the way it would have to be!

For more than 20 or 25 minutes Tom kept yelling for Officer Jackson to fuck him harder and harder. And Officer Jackson did try, but being in Tom's really hungry ass, —had actually hit Officer Jackson's upper limit. Fucking him as hard, as swiftly and as roughly as he could, he suddenly grabbed Tom by the chest and told him, "Hold on boy! I am going to unload everything up in you! I'm shooting, —I'm shooting, —oh shit man, —I'm cummmmin man, —I'm cumin!! Oh God man! You are one hot ass! Shit man, I have never fucked an ass as hungry as yours!"

Officer Jackson collapsed on top of Tom. He breathed very hard. He attempted to regain his breath. "Oh shit man! I am fucking worn out! Shit man, I thought you were afraid of taking my dick! Shit man, you sure were begging for it! Oh man alive! I hope you know you just got one big ass full of some ole Highway Officer's cum! Oh shit man, I let you have it!"

"Hey Tyler, you need to come fuck this one! Shit man, he has one hungry, hungry, horny, asshole! You know what Tyler? I think you need to come fuck this one, and then when you get done with him, I think we need to let his big brother try him out, too. As hungry as this ass is, I'm sure he will be ready to take it from his big brother, after you get done. Right Tom? You want Officer Tyler to do you, and then have your big brother find out how hot of an ass you've got? Right? Tyler, I think maybe it's time we teach these two brothers how to fuck around with each other and how to have some fun together. As hungry as this ass is, we need to make sure his big brother knows how to take care of it for him. He's obviously not getting that ass fucked as often as he needs. I think it might be fun to watch two brothers fuck each other for their very first time, don't you?"

CHAPTER THREE:

Let's Go Give Them a Show!

Officer Jackson left Tom strapped and chained down to the table, and he then went over and replaced Officer Tyler in his actions of taking care of Jim.

"Go get in the ass of that one over there on the table." Jackson said to his co-fucking companion, Officer Tyler. "He's still real "ass hungry", and from the way he is acting, I think he is wanting another dick up in his ass as quickly as you can get it up in there."

"Okay, you take over here on this one." Tyler replied. "He's not gotten it in the ass yet, but let me tell you something, if he even tries half as hard to take all of your dick like he has been on mine, you are going to have one hell of a happy dick stuck up in that guy's mouth. He loves to suck cock, and I'm sure he is going to love every bit of yours. He sure did suck mine to a complete and a very good final climax! He knows how to suck!"

"Hey good! I'm all for that! So Jim, you ready to take my big long black rod down your throat and make me one hell of a happy guy?" He asked Jimmy.

"I'm going to try, but Sir, you have got one hell of a big and long dick on you, and I will have to admit that I've never had a chance to try getting that much, shoved down my gut before. So all I can say right now is that I just hope I don't throw up trying to take it! I'm game and I'm real anxious to try, but I've got to admit that I've never tried anything close to being that big."

"Jim, my boy! I am sure you are going to do just fine on it. A lot of guys have begged me before, to not even try sticking it in their mouths, then all of a sudden they were begging for more once they finally decided to go for it. Of course, maybe their deciding to go for it was more of a forced, —"go for it." I've had to literally sit on a number of faces to hold them down long enough to get it started in their mouths. Some of them are real anxious to take it up in their asses, but scared like shit to think about taking it down their throats. I'm going to lay down here on my back and just let it stick up in the air. You get yourself up on top of me, and as long as I think you are really trying, I'll just let you take your time. Put that dick in your mouth and start sucking on it boy! You know damn well that you want it, all of it and you will do whatever you need to do to get it! Right? Suck on it boy!"

Jim immediately straddled Officer Jackson's body as the officer laid down and so very politely presented his rock hard, stiff, hard-on to Jim for his acceptance. Jim started his pleasure trip by first putting his tongue on Officer Jackson's right ankle and so very slowly and so very lovingly licked his way up from this ankle, to his knee, then into the inside of the officer's upper leg and eventually to the base of his large black, nut filled bag. After enjoying the soft texture of the bag and also the movement of feeling Officer Jackson's large balls move around inside of his velvet bag, Jim then repositioned himself and repeated the same venture starting from on his left ankle. Slowly and very deliberately, Jim made genuine love to the muscular and strong thick legs of this officer.

As Jim moved so slowly up the entire length of Officer Jackson's legs, the officer exclaimed, "Oh shit man! Oh shit, —do you know how to love a man's legs! Oh Jim, you feel so good! Kiss my bag man, —kiss my bag!"

Hearing the instructions, or possibly the begging, for more tender attention, Jim did as he was asked to do. He moved his face right up to the bottom of Officer Jackson's bag and slowly and lovingly he kissed the soft flexible skin. He kissed it twice, then three times and then very lovingly he sucked the officer's left ball into his mouth. He rolled that ball around and sucked on it with great care that he did not clamp down on it too tightly. He then got the other ball all positioned, so that he could suck it into this mouth, also. As soon as he did, Jim realized that he had a very full mouth full. Very full! His attempts of moving the balls around in his mouth simply did not work. His mouth was just too full! Mentally he thought, "Oh my God! They are coconuts!"

Having this feeling of almost more of a mouthful than he could actually manage, made him very excited and all of a sudden he felt his already hard dick, stretch out even farther. Suddenly he wanted the big muscular officer's dick in his mouth, and he knew this was going to be a big problem for him, but a problem that he was now anxious to take.

Slowly and carefully he expelled the officer's right ball, and then after rolling the remaining left ball around in his mouth for a few minutes, he then let it slide out and with one smooth movement, he took a very deep breath and repositioned himself so that his mouth was immediately at the tip of the enormous cock.

Jim opened his mouth, took another very concentrated deep breath, and actually threw his mouth down onto the dick as firmly as he could! He managed to get just about one half of its length into his mouth. He steadied himself, he took another deep breath, and with grabbing the hips of his hunky officer, he tried as much as he could to relax the back of his throat so that he could force more of that dick down into his mouth and deep into this throat!

Officer Jackson knew that Jim was anxious, horny, and very ready to take all of his dick, if at all possible, but he also knew that he was going to need to be patient with Jim if he was going to let Jim be successful in taking the entire length.

Jim's eyes watered, and he rather moaned, but he managed to demonstrate to Officer Jackson that he really was game in trying to take the entire length. Jim knew that he may never have another chance like this to take this much dick, and he certainly was not willing to let this session end without his every attempt of taking every little bit of it that he could. He knew that the length was a major obstacle, but he was even more sure that the enormous girth of it was creating its own challenges. Jim knew it was very fat, or maybe, not fat, but rather very muscular, and it was not until later, during some conversations all based on his attempts to take the whole dick, that he found out that the dick that he was currently sucking on measured a little more than six inches around, and the crown of it was even thicker!

Officer Jackson knew that he was involved in a very good sex scene, one that included a big muscular, highway patrolman,— just laying on his back, offering his enormous hard, thick, long, black, dick to another man, and this was probably the hottest gay sex scene that could be imagined. But to him, this was much more! It was the scene of him, a human being, offering to another human being, something that is not normally offered, and something that the other human being is having trouble taking to his complete satisfaction. And that being, the overly large and overly thick man-dick that the other man wants so very badly put down his throat, as completely and as thoroughly as possible. Officer Jackson did now, feel like he was being an instrument of a non-human form, offering to the other man something that could not be available, anywhere else, and for that other man to use, —to his complete sexual enjoyment and excitement! He truly did feel as if he was giving his sucker, the experience that maybe only one or two people, ever get the chance to try! And that enjoyment, and that experience being, that he had accomplished his mental goal of getting that much man-meat, man-cock, thrust down his throat.

Officer Jackson knew he was now part of something, for somebody else, that was completely unexplainable. He was the object of an act that his partner of sex could not find anyplace else, or with anybody else. He knew that offering his large rigid stick to Jim, for Jim's enjoyment and accomplishment, was an act of almost unbelievable proportions. He knew Jim could not accomplish what he was wanting to do, with any other person, or any other cock, and probably any other officer! Officer Jackson knew that he needed to just lay there and let Jim do whatever he was capable of doing, and in whatever time it took for Jim to succeed in his attempts. He wanted Jim to succeed and feel proud of his accomplishments. And, —he wanted to know, that yes, —he had actually put his entire dick down into that guy's mouth! All of the way!

Jim grabbed, hugged and squirmed on top of Officer Jackson in his unconscious attempts to eat as much of that man as he possibly could. Jim had never, in all of his previous sexual actions, been this consumed in getting so much man meat into his own body as he was this night! He had almost been kidnapped from off of the highway, and now he was so excited that this whole episode had happened, that he was yelling within his own mind that he wanted the officer to get much more physically active with him, and to force all of that dick down into him without him having any control at all, over what happened or how it happened. Jim wanted the entire cock down his throat, and he wanted to become almost permanently planted on the front of Officer Jackson's body. He wanted to be an extension of Officer Jackson. He wanted that dick so far down in him, that being an extension of that gorgeous body, was the best way he could even think to himself of what he was really wanting. He wanted to become a part of Officer Jackson!

With more pressure with each attempt, Jim forced his mouth down and onto Officer Jackson's big stiff cock just a little farther each time. As he was completely consumed with his actions on the big stick, he unconsciously, but very lovingly, reached up and found both of the officer's tits, and with gentle care and love, he caressed each tit. His gentle care contrasted in a great comparison with his aggressive action on the officer's dick, and his attempts to swallow all of it. His complete mental attention was directed to his extreme desires of taking the entire length of the dick, and his careful loving of the officer's chest and tits was an extra that he was not even aware of. He was not even aware that he was touching anything other than the dick of his desire. He was completely engrossed in eating all of the ten inch long cock.

Officer Jackson enjoyed the actions that were taking place with his body, and he simply knew from Jim's actions that Jim did not know that he was unconsciously playing with his tits and his chest. Officer Jackson knew that Jim was in a "different world," just trying to make sure that he would finish up successful in getting all of that big black dick as completely down his throat as was possible. Officer Jackson knew that no other man had ever been so determined to take all of his hard rod, as Jim was this night. As he laid there, with Jim on top of him, and eating his dick with such determination, he was extremely glad that he had made the false traffic stop out on the interstate. To him, things were working out very well. He and Tom had already struck up a very good friendship, and from the way Jim was taking care of his horny needs, it certainly did look like he and Jim would be striking up a very close relationship also. Secretly he was now hoping that perhaps the two Ohio boys could possibly stay around, for the next two days, so that he and Officer Tyler could enjoy their actions, and their bodies, while they were off of work for the week-end.

As Jim very successfully reached his success point, his lips securely placed on the very base of the officer's big rod, Officer Jackson then rubbed him on the head and said, "Hey man! You are one good mid-western cock sucker! Jim, you have got all of my dick down your throat and I sure haven't seen you throw up yet. Didn't think you could do it, did you?"

Jim looked up toward the officer and shook his head, "No."

"Jim, I'm afraid that if you keep sucking on me much more right now, you are going to make me shoot my wad, and I don't want to do that just yet. Why don't we go over there with Tyler and Tom and see if Tyler can get out of Tom's ass long enough for you to find out just what it's like to fuck your own brother. I want to watch you two fuck each other. I've never seen two brothers go to each other for the first time before, and right now that idea is a real turn on to me. Can we do that?"

Jim slowly pulled back and finally off of the officer's big dick and replied, "Yeah, but let me just lay here for a minute and re-catch my breath. Man, trying to take that much dick down my mouth has about worn me out. I like sucking dick, but man, when it is that damn big, it is rough going. Man, sucking on that thing is about like sucking on the exhaust pipe of some truck! Just about that fucking big!"

"Okay Jim boy, lay there and get yourself all together. I'm going over there and see what's happening."

Officer Jackson got up, with a ragging hard-on still in place, and approached the table where Officer Tyler was still fucking the hell out of Tom's ass.

"Hey man! Haven't you hit China with that dick of yours yet?" He jokingly asked Tyler as Tyler was slamming Tom's ass with every bit of might that he had.

Officer Tyler stopped, almost in mid stroke, and looking at Jackson said, "Shit man! I have never, and I do mean never, including you, have I ever been in some guy's ass that keeps begging for more and harder like this guy does. Shit man! I figure that since you had already fucked this ass before I got in it, that he'd probably be a little sore and kind of want to go slow. Man, I am fucking exhausted! This kid has got to get his ass fucked more often than what he is getting, I sure can see that. He is one damn hungry horny kid!"

"I know!" Jackson answered. "I know what in the hell you are saying. Shit man. He wore me out when I was on his ass. He loves to get it up in the ass good and strong and deep and fast."

"Did you hear him yelling at me to fuck him harder? Every time I slammed that asshole, he yelled for more, harder, deeper! Damn his insides should be sore and raw!"

"Yeah Tyler, I could hear you two guys over here going after it. I knew he was about to wear you out the way he kept screaming for more. Hey, why don't you pull out of him and give him just a minute or two rest, like yeah, —let him get all hot and horny, —and then I wanna watch ole Jim boy do him. I've never seen two brothers fuck each other for the very first time, and right now that is really getting me all turned on. I know, it will probably be just like any other time two guys fucking, but just the idea that they are blood brothers, and they have never been in each others asses yet, is a real turn on."

"Hey Tom" Officer Jackson said toward Tom. "Hey guy, you want me to untie you and let you get up and maybe go use the shower room before we let your big brother fuck your ass? You do still want that, right? You want Jim boy to fuck you for the first time, right?"

"Oh yeah I do. Did you ask him if he's willing to do that? Do you know for sure he'll fuck me?"

"Well, I did not exactly ask him, but when I mentioned it to him and told him that I wanted to watch that happen, he sure did not object." Then turning toward Jimmy, Officer Jackson looked at Jimmy with a question expression on his face as if to ask, "You are going to fuck him, right?"

Jim was laying there on his stomach, attempting to re-coup some strength and he looked at Officer Jackson, understood what he was rather asking since he could hear the talk, and the conversation on the other side of the room, and he shook his head, "Yes."

"Hey Tom my boy! Your brother just told me that yeah—he is going to fuck your ass! Here, I'm going to undo you so you can go use the shower room and get yourself all ready to have a good family reunion. Officer Tyler and I are going to get to watch two brothers fuck each other for the very first time, and that is a real hot turn on to me. When you get done in the shower room, come back in here and if you want to be chained back down before Jim gets on you, we'll do that. If you'd rather not be tied down, that's okay too."

Officer Jackson un-strapped one side of the table straps and Officer Tyler undid the other side. They each helped Tom get up and off of the table. He had gotten very stiff from laying on the table, without much body movement, except for the fast actions that had been going on in his ass.

Officer Jackson then told Tom, "Come on boy. I'll show you where the shower room is. Hey Jim, do you want to go use the shower room too?"

Jim did not answer but did get up so that he could go with Officer Jackson and Tom.

The barn was no longer used as part of a farm, but had been converted into a "party" barn where companies could rent it out and have parties or events in it. The property had been in the Jackson family for a long time, and when the farm land was sold away from it, Todd Jackson, the Officer Jackson, bought the house and the barn and made the conversion into making the barn available to rent, for parties or maybe company employee events. Part of the conversion, included this playroom, —which was of course, a very secret room, and definitely not included as part of any event rental, and in addition, a very well equipped rest room arrangement for both the men and the women. The men's room did include a steam room and a shower room. These additional amenities did come in very handy for some of the event rental times, but were originally included in the remodel, specifically for evenings such as this, —the very private evenings!

Officer Jackson showed the two brothers just where the shower room was, and where all of the equipment was stored, such as the douching hoses, if either one wanted to douche, and he then returned to the playroom, and some conversation with his buddy Tyler!

Jim and Tom turned on two of the shower heads that were available. The gang shower did have four shower heads. As Tom looked around he commented, "For a rest room in a barn, sure is nice, isn't it?"

"Jim replied that he agreed, and then looked at his brother and commented. "Well, Tommy guy. We've been pretty good brothers, but I guess tonight is bringing us a lot closer together than we have ever been before. Have we lived in kind of some shelter environments or something? Tonight is the first time that either one of us has really let our hair down, so to say, and let the other one know what he was thinking. Tommy, I've never really ever thought about wanting to fuck you. I just always looked for some other guys. You really do want me to fuck you? Those officers are not making that up?"

"Yeah Jim, yeah, I want you to fuck me, and I've wanted that for a long, long time now. I've just been too afraid of what you might say if I told you, so I've never told you. Yeah, Jim, there have been many nights when I went to sleep with my finger up in my ass trying to make believe that was your dick. But, from what I have just found out about you tonight, if I was wanting to make believe that finger was your dick, I would have had to have had about four or five fingers up in there." Tom reached over and grabbed ahold of Jim's dick, stroked it a couple of times, and said, "Shit man, I had no idea that my big brother had such a damn big dick! Jim, your dick is enormous! God, it feels good, man! I want it up in my ass!"

"Hey thanks brother, but you got that Officer Jackson's dick slammed up your ass already tonight, and compared to that one, mine is really kind of small, don't you think?"

"Well, —yeah Jim, but compared to his, I think every other dick is pretty small. But man, if I can get you into fucking my ass, and hopefully on a pretty regular and steady basis, your dick will do just fine. Knowing that I can get my brother's cock rammed up in my ass just about as often as I need it, will make be one happy camper! Jim, I've got to admit, I love to get fucked, and I like it good and hard. I want you to fuck me as hard as you can, and harder than you have ever fucked any of your buddies. I'm about all rinsed off here. You about ready to go back out there and show those two big hunky highway cops what two brothers can do, —when they finally decide to fuck each other? Let's go give 'em a show!"

CHAPTER FOUR:

Time to Consummate This Brotherhood

Jim and Tom left the shower room and went back into the playroom.

"Oh shit!" Tom said to Jim as they went into the playroom and found Officer Jackson sucking on Officer Tyler's dick, as Officer Tyler sat in the sling, with his legs up in the air, held up by the sling chains.

"Come on in boys!" Officer Tyler said as he watched the two brothers enter the room. "We've been waiting for you, but while we waited, Jackson here, decided that he needed some dick to suck on, so here we are! Give us a minute. I've got a hard stiff boner that needs some attention, and we'll be done in a minute."

Officer Jackson was sucking on Officer Tyler's dick as Officer Tyler laid in the sling, laying back, his dick up in the air, and his legs up along the chains that the sling hung from. Neither Jim nor Tom had watched a man get his cock sucked, while he was in a sling and they were both amassed at how exciting and fun it all looked. All Officer Jackson had to do was to stand there, in one spot, and kind of push Officer Tyler back and forth. As Officer Tyler swung back, his dick would, of course, come out of Officer Jackson's mouth, and then as he swung back forward again, he'd fuck his buddy's anxious mouth.

Officer Jackson turned as much as possible to look toward the brothers when he heard his buddy Tyler speak to them. He swung Tyler out and back just a few more times when he then stood up and said, "Hey buddy! I'll suck on this rod of yours, some more, later, but right now, we've got a brother fucking session to get under way, and as much as I love to have that dick in my mouth, this fuck is one that I do not want to miss. I do not know why, but the idea of watching these two brothers fuck each other for the very first time, is really turning my bells on."

Then as he helped Tyler out of the sling, Officer Jackson turned to Jim and Tom and asked. "Guys, —neither one of you have ever sucked on your brother? Right? I mean, yeah, I already understand that Tom is, and has been real anxious to get fucked by you, Jim, but neither one of you two have ever sucked on the other guy?"

"No officer, we just never have." Jim replied. "Yeah, I've played with a lot of other guys, well maybe not a lot, but some, and for some funny reason I guess I just felt like playing with my brother was way off base. Yeah, —sure yeah, I do admit that there have been times when I really wanted some action, and I kind of thought that maybe, just maybe we could do it, but then all of a sudden I went back to my old ways of, —no, —he's my brother!"

As Jim spoke the words, 'I kind of thought that maybe, just maybe we could do it', Tom immediately flipped his head toward Jim and said, "Well shit man! Damn if I had ever thought that you had even played with the idea of you and me doing each other, man I'd have been fucking all over you! Jim, I have admired your body ever since high school days, and man, yeah, I have wanted to, so many times to tell you that I wanted you to fuck me, but shit man, I guess I just never thought that you would go for that. And brother, —if I had known before tonight, what in the hell you have been hiding in your pants, I know damn well I would have raped you just to get to that damn thing! Jim, why in the hell were we so up-tight with each other that we couldn't do some fun stuff with each other, —like I'm sure other brothers do. Shit man, I wish we would have gotten started a long time ago. Jim, it's not like we could have kids together or anything. We're just two guys that like to fuck around with other guys. Why in the hell weren't we doing it? We both know we both like guys!"

"Tom I guess maybe it was either the way we were raised or something that we were told when we were young kids, or just that I always had my buddies and you had yours. Tom, I don't know why. Kid, I will tell you though, —that right now I am really thankful for these two guys that pulled us over. As kinky as it was! You know, they always say, —there's always a reason for stuff. Well right now, I think the reason we got picked off of the highway, wasn't so much so these two hunky guys could get their rocks off using us, but somebody up there, wanted to give you and me a reason to finally get it on together. Tom, I've sneaked peaks at you when you were getting in the shower or maybe undressed sometimes, but I just never had the guts to tell you that I wanted to punch that ass. Yeah, man, my rod, the one that you think is so damn big, is big, because I've jerked on it enough times and part of those times was thinking about how hot your ass looked. Tom, Officer Jackson and Officer Tyler have become our guardian angles tonight, and tonight I am going to fuck your ass, my little brother's ass, right in front of our angles."

Officer Jackson grabbed Jim, spun him around and gave him a bear hug. Jim hugged back and said, "Man, I am so damn glad you guys picked us tonight. I love having sex with both you and Officer Tyler, but man, you really don't know how many times I've wished there was some way that I could tell my brother how I wanted to fuck his ass, or maybe have him fuck mine. But we just never talked to each other that way." Then as Jim looked into Officer Jackson's eyes, he added, "Thank you man! Thank you! You two guys have finally brought two brothers together! Thanks!"

As they broke their hug, Officer Jackson and Jim realized that, as they were hugging, so were Tom and Officer Tyler. As they broke their hug, Officer Tyler looked at Tom and asked. "Okay man! The time has come! We've had almost enough emotions on display here for a few minutes, it's time to consummate this brotherhood. Tom, what do you want? You want to get fucked, or you want to fuck your brother?"

"Oh man! Oh shit! Just to hear those words spoken is a real anxious turn-on, to me. Why is playing with my brother such a rush? Man, I guess this is one of the reasons why we have never done each other. Just the going over the fence and getting into another playing field, is a real rush! Does that make any sense? But that's the way I feel right now. I've watched Jim put his whole face down on both of your cocks, and he's heard me screaming for more dick up in my ass and asking for you guys to give it to me harder, but the idea that it is finally time for me to get to do stuff with him, that is a real rush to me, man! I want him to fuck me! Jim I want you to fuck me! Oh man! Wow, I never thought I'd ever hear me say those words. Yeah, Jim, I want you to fuck me! Wow, I still can't believe I said that! Okay? Then after you fuck me, I'll fuck you if it's okay with these two guys! Okay?"

"Yeah Tom, yeah that's okay with me! Tom, this is a rush to me too. I don't understand why it is, I mean like you said, —we've watched each other have sex with these two hot guys, but the idea that it will be you and me, why, why-oh-why,—is that such a funny rush to me? Shit man! Yeah Tom, lay down, I want to fuck your ass! There, I finally said it! Like you said, you never thought you would ever say those words. Well that is exactly the way I feel right now. Tom, I want to fuck your ass! God, I can't believe this! Neither one of us even watched the other guy have sex, with anyone before, and now we've watched each other have sex with other guys, and now I am telling him I want to ram my cock up in his ass! Oh God, I am so damn glad you pulled us over! "

"Okay Tom, come over here." Officer Jackson said. "Here guy, lay down here on the table. Tom do you want to be strapped and chained back down like you were before?"

Before Tom had a chance to answer, Jim spoke up. "Yeah, he's going to be tied down. Yeah, I saw you do that to him earlier, and that really turned me on! Yeah I want to tie him down on his stomach and can we use one of those blindfolds that you have over there? I want him blindfolded."

"Yeah of course!" Officer Jackson said. "Shit man! I already told you guys that just the mental idea of watching you two brothers go to it for the first time is a real turn on to me, but Jim, your instructions of wanting him tied down and also blindfolded is really getting me all hot and bothered. And in a big way!"

"Well, I've got to agree with that!" Officer Tyler said. "Jackson, I told you while we were at the department, turning in the cruisers, that I had some real doubts about these two, and if we were going to have much fun with them. I really did think they were kind of, on the too tame side, but shit man, I guess it's the old saying, —don't judge a book by its cover. Jackson, during this whole night, whenever you said how excited you were about getting to watch these two do it to each other for the first time, it never really made any sense to me. I thought, well shit, guys do each other for the first time everyday. Before Jim boy here spoke up, and said, he did not suggest or ask, he said, that Tom boy would be tied down and blindfolded, I thought okay, another fuck session, but after that statement, I'm into this! Jackson, I understand your excitement now! Shit man! Look at the boner I'm hanging. And I know damn well it's all over Jim taking total control over how he treats his kid brother. Man, I'm all turned on now, too! Shit man! Jackson, these two are turning out to be the best two you have every stopped. I thought that guy that was totally bare assed when you pulled him over was good, but man, these two are such a happy shock to me, I've got to say they are the best. Jackson, you did good! Come on Jim, fuck your kid brother!"

Officer Tyler removed the tube of K-Y from the shelf, and after putting some on his own hand, he then offered it to Officer Jackson. Officer Jackson reached down and fully coated Jim's hard-on with the lube. Officer Tyler slightly spread Tom's ass cheeks, and gave Tom's asshole a complete coating of lube, and for just a slight moment before he removed his hand, he let Tom feel two fingers go up into, his soon to be fucked, hole! Tom smiled and turned toward Officer Tyler and simply said, "Thanks, man! Thanks!"

Officer Jackson helped Tom up on the padded table, stretched him out and started chaining him down. Officer Tyler got one of the black blindfolds from the beg board. As he returned to the table, Officer Tyler placed the blindfold on Tom's face, made sure it was well positioned, then bent over and gave him a kiss on the cheek and said, "We love you man! We are going to watch your big brother take your ass for his first time. You ready? You want fucked by your big brother, right? You ready?"

"Oh shit yes, I am! Oh God yes! Oh God! Thanks guys! I've dreamt of this day for years now! Oh shit man, I'm actually going to get fucked by my big brother! I can't believe it is actually happening! Hey guys, thanks for making this happen!"

Tom could not see what was happening since he was blindfolded, but he certainly could tell that somebody, and he had to assume that it was his brother, that was licking his legs from down by the ankle, and was slowly moving his way up. He anxiously laid there just giving himself the metal picture of what it must look like for his brother, to be laying down, with his face so close to his bare ass as he licked his way up his legs, then take a small bite out of his left hip before he then moved on up and started licking around his waist.

Tom laid there and completely and very happily accepted the attention that he was now finally getting from his older brother. He felt like all of his previous days of feeling like he did not matter, were now gone. He had suffered so many days when he simply knew that his brother was having sex and making love to some other guy, when Tom really wanted to be the one in bed with him. Tonight it was all happening! He was chained down to the bed, and he was being licked, up one side and down the other, by his brother! He had actually felt his brother's face move up, between the insides of his legs and he had felt his brother's tongue on his bag. His big brother had actually licked his bag!

Jim had worked his way up Tom's left leg, across his butt, down the right leg and then back up to lick and caress Tom's waistline and his lower back. Jim had then worked his way up to Tom's shoulders, and Tom knew that his brother was now licking on the base of his neck.

As he simply enjoyed this very new and very exciting experience, he realized that he was also being licked by both of the other two men in the room.

One man, which one he did not know, was licking on his left butt cheek and the other man was sucking on his right butt cheek. Tom knew that although he could not see the action, he was now being played with by all three men. He knew it was his brother, up by his neck, but he did not know if it was Officer Tyler or Officer Jackson that was sucking some of his butt cheek into his mouth. He really did not care who was doing what, all he knew was that he had never had anything, like this experience, happen to him. He felt like he was the center of the entire world! He was in bliss! He was in glory! He wanted to yell out to the world that he was being used and he was being tasted by three men, and he loved it. One man was his brother, one that he had lusted over for years, although he had never been able to have sex with him, and the other two men were hot looking highway patrolmen. One officer, that really looked like some movie star, was about as muscular of a man as any person could imagine, and the other officer was another very muscular strong man, that just happened to be a very nice mahogany colored man.

Tom had read many, many, gay stories of how white guys get a chance to make it with a big strong black man, and right now he was that little white guy. Not only was his black god built like a brick shit house, he was also a highway patrol officer, and just like all other officers, his uniform pants hugged and loved his legs to the point that any straight guy would drool in envy, of just being able to look that hot, even with clothes on. As Tom laid there and enjoyed his position of being the main, and the only, item of attention from the three other men, he remembered just how hot and damn hunky those two officers were, out by the highway, when they were doing their pat downs. Tom remembered that when he was being patted down, Officer Jackson had felt his hard-on and had made it harder by rubbing his hand across it, back and forth about four or five times. He now had that same officer, either licking on his skin, or maybe, he was the officer that was sucking some of his butt skin into his mouth. Whichever officer it was, that was doing that to his butt, he definitely did enjoy the feeling of it, and what was happening. He could feel the man's mouth suck in his skin, and then he could feel a tongue sweep across it and take a taste from it.

Tom just knew, that with the joy and the excitement that he was experiencing here, in the middle of the three other men, he could only wish, that after he had been patted down, out beside the open highway, that he had realized fast enough, of just what was going on, so that he could have suddenly turned to the officers and do an aggressive pat down of them, —both of them! The mental image of him, standing out by the open highway, giving a highway patrolman a good pat down, rubbing his hands across the officer's dick, like they had done to his, was making Tom's heart pound. Oh, how he would have loved for cars to go flying by and then have those people realize that they had just seen some guy, rubbing the inside of a patrolman's upper legs. How many times had he lusted over the idea of just being able to reach out and slightly touch the tight pulled fabric, that so hugged and kissed the crotch area and the inside of an officer's upper leg! Just laying there and thinking about that possibility made Tom drop some per-cum out of his raging dick! His wishes and desires of what he now wishes, could have happened, out by the highway, and the actions of being played with by three guys, his older brother, and two hot cops, was creating his most exciting time of his life, that he had ever lived!

Tom knew that somehow, some way, before they left the farm, he simply needed to find one chance to do a complete rub down of both of the officers and their hot slick uniform pants. He wanted to feel the inside of their legs so badly! Officer's uniform pants, and the way they hugged every muscle of a patrolman's lower body parts had been a complete and exciting turn-on to Tom ever since his earliest of junior high days, and now that he had two officers licking and sucking on him, and a brother that would not think anything funny about doing it, he knew he had to take this chance to finally feel the upper inside of an officer's legs, while he was wearing a pair of his tight, tight uniform pants. Somehow, he had to do that! Somehow before they left, he had to have a chance to tell the two officers of how he wanted to rub his hands and his face, up in the upper part of their uniform pants. He decided that the officers had to already know how gay guys have always talked about wanting to do that, and how he really was one that needed to do it. "Please!" He pleaded to himself, as if he was now asking for the permission to lick one of their legs.

All of a sudden, Tom felt his brother's body lay across him. Jim completely laid down on Tom. He reached up under Tom's arm pits and placed his hands up and then over behind Tom's neck. He clasped his hands together. That pulled the two brothers up tight, very tightly together.

"Oh shit, oh man!" Tom exclaimed! "Oh Jim I can feel you all over me! Oh man, I've finally got my brother on me. Oh Jim, hug me!"

Jim did as Tom had asked, but it was not a result of Tom's asking. It was the natural action for one brother, that was now completely skin to skin to his younger brother. A brother that was stretched out, under him, totally bare, and chained down.

"Oh yeah! Oh yeah! Oh Tom you feel so good to me man! Oh Tom, oh Tommy!" Jim was feeling some extreme emotions of excitement in being skin to skin to his younger brother. A feeling that he had wanted for years, but for some stupid reason had never let it be known.

Officer Jackson and Officer Tyler stood off to the side watching with eyes wide open to the love that was now taking place between the two brothers that had always been around each other, but had never taken the opportunity to really let the other brother know what the true feelings were. Tom had admitted that he had dreamt for years about having this happen, and Jim had admitted how he had sneaked peaks at his kid brother's bare ass, but never had the guts to tell him how he wanted to punch it, and now, finally after way too many empty years, of each secretly wanting and wishing, the two brothers were finally, completely naked, one brother tied and chained down, and the other brother completely laying across him. Both men were feeling the great joys of having his bare skin touching his brother's bare skin.

The two officers, —but not really looking much like officers at this time, since they were both complete nude and both men were supporting ragging hard-ons, were arm in arm, watching the two brothers enjoy this first time experience.

Before Officer Jackson started the sucking session on his buddy Tyler, as they waited for the two brothers to re-emerge from the shower room, he had dimmed the lights in the playroom to a much softer level, and he had lit three candles that were very strategically placed around the room.

The soft light of the room, the flickering of the candles, the emotions being emitted from the two brothers, and the very strong love of each other between Jackson and Tyler, created an essence of complete male bonding and love, being shared by all of the men in the room at that time. Jackson hugged Tyler, but said nothing. Tyler silently returned the hug, looked into Jackson's face and smiled. They shared their own personal feelings for each other as the two brothers, unknowingly, provided the correct setting for that simple and loving exchange.

Silently and without saying anything, even to Tyler, Officer Jackson internally grinned to himself and compared the contrast, of this love session on the padded table, to some of the much more wilder and untamed sessions that had taken place in that very same spot. Sessions that certainly could not be referred to in any fashion as a love exchanged, but much more as a true power struggle between two or more men. Men that were reaching for the ultimate high and rough level of ragging gay sex!

Jackson thought, "What a contrast! One night that table can be the center of actions that most people could never accept as normal or natural behavior between two or three men, and then on a night like tonight, complete love and sharing between two brothers! If that table could talk!"

The exchange happening on the table was a true expression of togetherness that had been avoided for way too many years. Silently and almost without any movement, Tom and Jim were completely accepting the new bonding and the relationship between them, and each man was internally, and emotionally excited that he now finally had his brother as close to him as was possible. Nothing, not even a piece of clothing separated these two men. They were completely together, and only one more act could bring them any closer at all, and that was, of course, for Jim to put his large cock-rod up inside of his brother.

Tom so very quietly and pleadingly said, "Oh Jim, fuck me, please! Please put it up in me! Jim, let me know you are in me! Jim, I want you up inside of me!"

Jim raised his torso enough to aim his rod directly toward his brother's asshole. He slid his hard-on between the cheeks of Tom's ass. As he separated the muscular butt cheeks, he let out a very excited moan as he felt his own cock start to slide in between the cheeks of his brother's ass.

"Oh man! Oh man! Tom, I'm about to fuck your ass! You ready? Tom, I'm going to fuck you!"

"Yeah man, yeah! Yeah, Jim. Put it in me! Please push it in my ass!"

Suddenly Jim pushed down, and completely rammed his brother's ass!

"Oh God yes! Oh God yes!" Tom almost screamed in joy and excitement. "Oh God! Jim you are finally fucking me! Oh shit man! I can't believe it! You are finally up in me! You are finally fucking me! Oh Jim, fuck me hard! Real hard!"

Watching Jim slam down into Tom's ass, was almost more than either Officer Jackson or Officer Tyler could stand. Immediately both men started jerking off. Both men got so excited in watching the brothers finally fuck, and finally put their bodies together, that both men immediately lost all self control over their own actions.

Officer Jackson almost screamed on his own. "Oh my God man! Oh shit! Fuck him! Oh Jim fuck his ass! Fuck him hard man! Jim your brother wants to feel your cock up inside of him, fuck him man!"

Officer Tyler was not left out of the visual and emotional excitement. He too was yelling, "Oh man, fuck your brother! Fuck his ass! Fuck him hard! Show us how much he can take from his brother! Fuck him, fuck him!"

As the two officers watched the two brothers fuck, listen to Jim moan and groan in total joy and pleasure, as he punched his brother's ass, and as they listened to Tom continually yell for, "More, harder, fuck me harder," they took their own actions to hand.

Tyler grabbed Jackson by the arm and quickly turned him around and rather threw him up against the wall, and without so much as a question of "Ready?" he slammed his stiff dick up and into Jackson's ass.

With Jackson pushed up against the wall, and with Tyler boring his ass as if it had never been fucked before, the two hunky cops escaped into a completely different 'space' of one man taking the ass of his friend, and that friend offering his ass back to his horny friend. Offering was not quite the way Jackson saw it as Tyler's big stick went in, especially since that stick had absolutely no lube on it, but, none the less, after it made its forced entry, and the sudden shock and pain had subsided, Jackson was more than eager to let his buddy use it for a quick and convenient place to drop his cum shots.

It did take only a moment for Tyler to hit his point of no control, and with every imaginable muscle and bit of strength that he had, he pushed Jackson up against the wall and loaded his ass with his warm, white, baby producing cum, and tried over and over to make more cum shoot. He knew he was done shooting, but the act of forcing his patrol buddy friend, up against the wall, to where he had actually no control, was way to hot of an episode for Tyler to withdraw from earlier than he had to. As he finally stopped, he leaned against Jackson and said, "Okay, now I know damn well that if you have a kid, it's mine! After that shot man, you should have a fucking litter of kids!"

Hearing the actions that were happening up against the wall added to Jim's excitement of finally fucking his kid brother.

"Tom, I'm getting real ready here man! Tom, do you want me to cum in your ass? Tom, I'm getting real close man! Tom, do you want it man?"

Hearing that question made Jackson and Tyler turn around and redirect their attention to the table and the fucking session that was going on there.

"Oh shit man, Jim's about ready to shoot man! Tyler, Jim's about ready to load Tom's ass! Oh God man! This is so damn hot to me! Oh man, one brother cumin in his own brother. Oh shit man! Why is that such a complete fucking turn on to me man? Tyler, why in the hell is that such a fucking turn on to me?"

Tyler immediately responded, "Hell, I don't know, but I do know that while you are getting this damned excited, you could be using that big telephone pole on something better than just your hand. Fuck me man! Come on, fuck my ass while Jim knocks his brother up!"

Tyler grabbed ahold of Jackson's dick and aimed it at his own hole. "Push man! Push! Come on Jackson, my ass is dry, you've got to push it in. I want your dry massive dick up in my ass! Fuck me! Fuck me!"

Even Jackson thought Tyler had to be a little, or maybe a whole lot out of his mind begging to get fucked by that enormous dick without any lube on it, but he had done it before, and Jackson decided that once again Tyler was so fucking turned on by the actions that were going on in the room, that he was wanting sex rougher and harder than usual, and getting Jackson's dry dick rammed up in his ass was about the most outrageous and exciting thing that he could do, to just try and fulfill his sexual desires right then.

Jackson pushed Tyler over toward the counter and made him lay his head down on the counter top. He took ahold of his ragging hard-on and positioned it right at the opening of Tyler's ass. "Hang on man! It's dry! I'm going to fuck you and you are going to feel it man! Here it comes!"

And with that statement, Jackson pushed his rod up and into Tyler's ass.

"God shit man!" Jackson said. "Shit man! My God Tyler how in the hell can you take it when it is dry? Shit man, it's not even my asshole and fucking you dry hurts my dick! Shit man, how in the hell can you take it?"

"Oh God you're in now, just fuck me! Come on buddy, just fuck me! Fuck my ass!"

This action was way too much for Jim to take and maintain any personal body control over. He had told his brother that he was about to cum, —Tom never said to pull out, and when Tyler insisted that Jackson fuck him dry, the screaming that Jackson let out when he forced his own dick up into Tyler, was the limit! The excitement was way too great! Right then is when Jim felt like he had just shot his first load, of anytime. He knew very well that he had shot many of a load before, and quite a number of them had been shot up into other guy's asses, but knowing that this was his first load into his brother's ass, simply made it more exciting to him than any cum shot he had delivered before!

As officer Jackson heard Jim squeal in complete excitement that he was cumin, and he told his brother to hold on man, "I'm cumin, I'm cummmmin man, I'm cummmin!" Officer Jackson told Officer Tyler, too. "Hold on man, I'm cumin! I'm cumin! Tyler, —Tyler you're taking my cum man, you're taking my cum! Have my kids, have my kids!"

Jim, in his brother's ass, and Jackson in Tyler's ass, and almost everybody screaming at the same time, either from the excitement of getting ready to cum, or the excitement of having one hell of a hot dick up in their asses, was more sexual excitement than either, he or Tom, had ever experienced. Both brothers were living in what they later termed, 'Sexual Heaven'!

Tom had finally been fucked by his brother! He was now finally getting it, and he was loving it!

As Jim and Jackson both attempted to re-gather themselves from the actions of servicing their respective bottoms, all four men recouped and mentally enjoyed the total joy and excitement that each one of them had just experienced.

"Jackson," Tyler said. "Jackson, try to tell me of a more exciting time, with any guy you can think of, that was more of a turn on than this night has been. Jackson, these two boys as the pinnacle of our sex sessions!"

"I know it Tyler! Shit man! When you threw me up against that wall and slammed your cock up in me, without saying anything, I knew you were way out there man! You never act that way! You always ask first, before you ram my ass or any other guy's ass. And then, when you wanted a dry fuck, I knew damn well you were really loosing it. Tyler, I've played with you before when you got all hot and bothered, but shit man, tonight was your highest! Never, and I do mean never, have I ever been around you when you got that damn hot for sex. Hell, I am usually the one that everybody says I get all too hot and bothered, but shit man, tonight you were the one! Is your ass okay after that dry fuck? You feeling okay?"

"Yeah my ass is okay. Yeah, it does feel kind of weird, but hey man, I've been dry fucked by you and that damned railroad tanker before and I didn't loose my ass, so I'm sure it will be okay tonight. I will tell you one thing though! I'm fucking tired! I think we got our use out of these guys, don't you Jackson? I'm ready for bed. It's late! I got up early today, and now I am pooped. What are you going to do about these two guys?"

"Well, I sure did not expect this little session to go on as long as it did, so I really think that the best thing is to just let them sleep here, in the barn for as long as they need to, and then they can hit the road whenever they want. Is that okay with you guys? You both know where the shower is and the towels and stuff that you might want to use, right? You know how to get back to the highway, don't you?"

"Uh yeah." Jim replied. "It's okay if we sleep here then? We can use the playroom for some sleep, and then hit the road whenever we wake up? Is that what you mean?"

"Yeah. I don't want you guys out on the highway this late." Officer Jackson told the brothers. "Tyler and I are going in and going to bed. You guys crash out here for awhile, and then hit the road whenever you feel like it, or when it starts getting light out. Just don't take anything from in here, Okay? Remember, I've got all of your information in case we need to come find your little ass to get something back. Oh, here Jim. Here's your driver's license back. Thanks for letting us have some fun, guys. Get some sleep. Tyler and I are out of here. Stop back and see us sometime if you are driving through again. Okay?"

Officer Tyler turned, grinned and said, "And, hey guys! Fuck each other as often as you can. Jim, that brother of yours needs a good stiff cock up his ass a little more often than what he's been getting. Fuck your brother!"

"Thanks guys!" Both Tom and Jim hollered as the two officers gathered up their uniforms and headed out the door and toward the house.

The brothers watched the two muscle cops walk hand in hand toward the house, and then closed the barn door. Tom looked at Jim, Jim looked at Tom, and then Tom said, "Brother, we have a lot of talking to do. I'm not going on to Denver! I don't know what you are doing, but I'm not going to Denver!"

CHAPTER FIVE:

This Time, Things Were Quite different!

The session and the evening before, had been much longer than what had been expected. Previously each time that Officer Jackson and Officer Tyler had managed to take some poor un-expecting guy to the barn, it had worked out rather okay, but only to the point where the two officers were none too reluctant to just let their piece of 'meat toy' hit the road, so that they could get on with some of their more exciting actions, just between themselves.

This time, things were quite different. The actions had been much more to the officer's liking, and thus, what is normally a one hour episode, on this occurrence it turned into about a three or four hour episode. What was normally a good seven or eight hours of sleep, had been cut short by about two or three hours, and as Officer Jackson and Officer Tyler awoke, they each felt the drag of not having quite enough sleep.

"Well good morning sir!" Officer Tyler said as he rolled over, and threw his arm across the chest of his co-officer bed mate. Officer Jackson slightly opened his eyes and peeked out.

"Yeah right, good morning. What time is it?" Was the sleepy reply, from the hot, hunky, and completely naked, officer that really was wanting to get some more sleep.

"It's about one half past, two —young horny brothers, —that we really took advantage of last night!"

"Oh yeah. Oh yeah! Yeah, that's why I feel like shit this morning! That was last night wasn't it? Yeah, I guess I thought that was a dream or something. Really, what time is it? I feel like it must still be in the middle of the night. Shit man, I'm tired and sleepy."

Officer Tyler, being considerably more awake and feeling much more playful than Jackson was, he over acted his attempts of looking at the clock, he completely threw himself up and across Jackson to look at the clock. Fortunately for him, and to his playful pleasure, the clock just happened to be on Jackson's side of the bed.

"Oh according to the little round face, on the little bedside clock, the big hand is on the two, and the little hand is on the eight, so I guess that must mean that we over slept!"

Officer Jackson's response was a quick, "I'm about to big hand you if you don't get off of me and let me get some more sleep! I'm tired! God, that session last night wore me out. Really, when I started waking up, I really did think it was some fuzzy dream I had, but it wasn't, was it? We really did have those two brothers here, didn't we? Shit man, that was fun! That was, without doubt, the best session we've ever brought home from the highway, wasn't it? Damn, that was fun! Now, let me roll over here and get some more snoozing in. I wanna sleep some more!"

"You can roll over okay, but unless you can sleep during one good morning fucking, you aren't getting anymore sleep. I'm still horny from last night, and I've got some more jazz up in me that really needs to get shot out, so I am going to fuck that cute little butt of yours until I can't hardly walk! Give me your ass man. I wanna fuck it!"

Not being the kind of a guy that will turn a good ass fucking down, especially when it is being offered by someone as hot as his buddy Tyler, Jackson threw off the sheet that he had been trying to roll up in, grabbed ahold of each side of his ass, pulled his cheeks apart and said, "Go for it, go for it!" Jackson had definitely come much more awake, and considerably less sleepy once he found out that Tyler was still horny and was wanting some early, well not too early, morning ass. His ass was always hungry and he knew it needed its morning breakfast, —of some Tyler!

"You want me to use some lube or you want a good dry skin to dry skin fucking man?" Tyler asked of his anxious and hungry bed mate.

"Dry! Fuck me dry! Just take your time. I like it better when it's dry. I can feel you up in me better that way! Just go in slow until I get you in there!"

Tyler slapped his hard-on dick up against Jackson's ass a couple of times, and then slowly pointed the tip of it directly at the body opening that Jackson was still holding open, and displaying with great anticipation. "Yeah man, here's my rod man! I love to fuck you! I love this! Hold that asshole open man! Let me put my rod up in there!"

Tyler pushed his cock up and into Jackson's ass, laid his full weight down onto Jackson and gave him a bear hug. "I love this man! I love this!"

"Me too! Tyler, me too! You feel so damn good in me. Man, I can only hope that when I fuck your ass, I feel as good to you as you do to me when you fuck mine! Oh man, I love to have you in me!"

"Oh yeah! Oh yeah!" Tyler rather quickly responded. "You dry fucked me last night, didn't you? Oh shit man, I forgot all about that! Shit man, I was so damned horny when those two brothers finally fucked each other, hell yes, now I remember I made you give me a dry fuck, didn't I?"

"Yes you did! Remember how I screamed about how it hurt my dry dick to push it up in you dry, —but shit man, I'm not even sure you felt it. You took it all, and totally dry!"

"Oh shit man! That was one hot night. Jackson, just that one brother got fucked didn't he? I mean by his brother. The younger one, —Tom, —yeah Tom, he got fucked by his older brother, but then Tom didn't fuck his brother, —right?"

"Yeah, I think the older one, Jim, yeah his name was Jim wasn't it? I think he wanted to fuck his brother, but it got so late, and we got tired and left the barn, so he didn't fuck him while we were there. I wonder if he fucked him after we came in here. I wonder what they did after we left. I hope they got some sleep before they left, though. It was late by the time we stopped, so I just hope they didn't leave right away. I hope they got some sleep. I told them to get some sleep and then hit the road. Wonder what time they left."

"I don't know." Tyler replied. "I don't know, but right now I will tell you that I wish we had found out more about them and maybe tried to see if they could have stayed over for another day or so. I loved fucking that younger kid. Shit man, he is one wild bottom. I mean, I love this fucking too, but after I get done with your ass, what a nice treat it would be to have his ass laying there, right beside this hot one, and then I could just use some of my left over cum, that I shot up in your ass, as a lube to use on his ass. Oh Jackson, why in the hell didn't we try to see if they could have stayed. Hell, we don't even know if they will be coming back through here on the way back to Ohio or not. Shit man! For us finding two hot assholes like those two are, we sure didn't play our cards too well about trying to get back together with them if possible."

"I know it Tyler! I thought about that last night just before we went to sleep. I guess it took me that long to kind of cool down and do some straight thinking! Yeah, you are right! I think we kind of screwed up there. As much fun as we had with them, we really should have found out more about them. Shit! Oh well! So we goofed! Hey, keep your eyes open for that car when you're on the road. Maybe we can find 'em again sometime. Now, fuck me man! Make believe I'm that Tommy guy, and fuck the hell out of me!"

"Well, if I'm going to make believe you are that Tommy guy, then we need to go to the barn and chain you down to that bench. Shit man, he liked that! You know Jackson, it was really fun playing with a couple of guys that had never been exposed to stuff like that before, but a couple of guys that did seem like they wanted to be a part of it."

Jackson turned his head as far as possible, since he was still getting it up in the ass, and said. "Yeah, you are right! Did you see the expression on that Jim's face when he saw us using the sling? I think he wanted to try that sling out. I think we could have gotten him in that sling if we had not come to bed. Shit man, —I wish we had done something about trying to see if they could have stayed. You know, from they way they were acting, I think that if we had mentioned it, —about them staying, they just might have! Course, we have no idea of where they were headed or how much time they had, but shit man, I agree, I wish we had done stuff differently. Shit man, we could have disabled their car some way, and then told them that no garages were open till Monday morning, and just not let them get off of the farm. Crap man! For us to take the chances that we do out there on the highway, with pulling guys off for no good reason, then kind of raping them, we sure don't follow through very well! Shit man, we really goofed! Damn I wish those two were still here and I hadn't told 'em to hit the road after they got some sleep."

"Well honey, I don't think you really told them to hit the road, you just told them to get some sleep first before they left."

"I know Tyler, but shit man, we didn't act like we wanted them to stay either! We goofed!"

Both men were less than pleased that they had not made some attempt to have the brothers hang around for a day or so. They agreed that for taking the chances that they do as Highway Patrol Officers, they sure let a good thing get out of their grip this time.

"The next time, it will be different! We learned from this one man! Next time, we'll know. Now fuck my ass! We can't lay here and cry in spilled milk about what we did or didn't do, we need to move on. Your dick is up in my ass, but I can't feel you moving it. Fuck me and fuck me hard! It's a new day!"

Tyler heard what had been said. He realized that in his sorrow of their not doing things differently, he had kind of stopped fucking, and was just laying on Jackson. He re-cooped his thoughts, and got back with the program. He knew damn well that he was already one lucky fellow to have a guy like Jackson available for him to use, and to be used by, and that was a pretty good thing. Yeah, the brothers had been fun, but he already had one, hot as hell, ass that was begging for some more action. He fucked Jackson! He fucked his buddy so good and so hard, that Jackson actually did have to ask him to kind of slow down a little. "God man, you are about to tear my ass out of me! Fuck me, but don't tear me up!"

"I'm sorry man! I just got all excited about realizing what I already had here to use, and I kind of got all excited. I forgot we were doing a dry fuck. Hey, Hon, I'm sorry!"

The two officers continued their Saturday morning fucking until suddenly Tyler got all excited, his body went rigid and he exclaimed, "Oh shit man, —I'm cumin! Oh man, —all of a sudden I'm there! Jackson, —I'm cumin man, —you're getting it man! I'm cummmin!"

After Tyler's climax, the two men, the two men that could easily be on the cover, naked and in bed together, of any gay mag, cuddled in each other's arms for a few minutes and then Tyler said that he needed to get up and go use the bathroom.

As he crawled out of bed, he stopped, turned, pulled the sheet back up over Jackson and asked him if he wanted to stay in bed a little longer and try to get some more sleep. Jackson told him, "Yeah, sounds like a good idea, but I doubt that I'll go back to sleep."

Tyler leaned over him, gave him a gentle kiss, and then turned to go to the bathroom.

As Tyler was leaving the bedroom, headed for the bathroom, he actually screamed out, "Oh my God! Oh my God, Jackson come here!"

Jackson jumped out of bed in somewhat of a panic since he had no idea of what in the hell Tyler was yelling about, and ran to the window where Tyler was standing.

"Oh shit! Oh shit man!" Jackson almost screamed as he looked out the window. "Shit man, they never left! That's their car! God Tyler! They are still here! My God Tyler, —they never left! Tyler, do you think they're still asleep?"

"Shit man, I have no idea! I figured they'd be long gone by this time. Shit man, grab some shorts or something, lets go see what happened! God man, I really thought they were probably long gone from here!"

The two officers grabbed some pants, did not bother with a shirt or shoes, and ran down the stairs and headed toward the back door, to go out toward the barn. As they quickly passed the dining room, Jackson suddenly stopped, Tyler ran into the back of him, and Jackson said, "Look! Look at the table! Tyler, it was not set like that! What in the hell is going on here? Tyler, I did not have the table set! What in the hell?"

Being terribly confused, Jackson turned, looked into the living room and found the two brothers calmly sitting there, totally nude, reading the morning newspaper, and looking over toward the two hot, muscular, and both very well hung officers, with very big grins on both of their faces!

Jim and Tom each looked toward the two very surprised and confused officers and Jim simply said, "Good morning men! Glad you are up. And we want to help you get it all up, again, —if you know what I mean!"

With their mouths hanging wide open, the two men entered the living room, looked at the brothers, and Jackson finally asked, "What in the hell is going on here? I am totally confused! What is going on?"

Jim spoke. "We decided to try and have as much guts as you two have, —when you take guys off of the highway and bring 'em here for sex. We decided that if you two could do that, then we could muster up enough courage to come in here, —in our birthday suits, —fix you guys a nice breakfast and talk some stuff over with you. Tom has everything ready to fix for breakfast, as soon as you two are ready. We did find a nicely supplied cupboard and refrigerator. This house is well supplied. Oh, you are out of orange juice though!"

Officer Jackson and Officer Tyler were in shock, and they admitted it.

"I'm completely beside myself!" Officer Jackson said. "Tyler, it's them! They are here! They never left!"

Tyler rather laughingly, replied, "Uh yeah! I know! Honey, I can see them. Yeah, it's them. Shit man! It's them! Honey, they are still here, and they are completely nude! Look at 'em! Look at how hot those guys are! Damn, did they look that hot last night?"

Jim then said, "Well men, —you two rather slept in this morning didn't you? It's getting kind of late. Or, was Tom right? He told me earlier that he thought he heard a bed squeaking up there. Like maybe someone was getting a Saturday morning fucking! Right?"

Jim and Tom then looked at the officers and grinned until Officer Tyler finally admitted that, "Yeah, I fucked his ass again! Shit man, —if I had known you two naked asses were down here, you guys would have gotten it too! I'd have fucked all three of you, I would have!"

The four men quickly hugged each other, and the two officers told the brothers how glad they were that they had not, in-fact, left and how excited they were to find them in the house. After just a few comments about how gutsy it was for the brothers to actually come on into the house and only hope that everything would be okay, and hoping that they would not be in trouble for doing it, Jim and Tom did jokingly tell the two officers that they felt that if anything did go wrong, they did have a pretty good story line that they could share with the highway department about two officers, —that do stop guys, —for no good reason at all, —and then take them to this barn, —and have sex with them.

Laughing as he said it, Tom said, "Payback's a shit you know!"

Jackson and Tyler both agreed completely with that comment! They definitely did not have any problem with the brothers being in the house, in fact they were over joyed about it, expressed their complete pleasure that the brothers had decided to present themselves in the nude, but they did agree that the brothers certainly could have used that story if things had not turned out as well as they had!

Tom told the officers, "Well, I think our main concern was, —does anybody else live here that could have come walking in while they were here in the nude? Hell, right now we don't even know for sure which one of you guys lives here, or do both of you?"

Officer Jackson explained that he lived there by himself, and Officer Tyler lived in town.

The officers told Tom, that since he was acting as the host, that they simply needed just a few minutes to shower and get a little more presentable, and they would then be ready for the surprise breakfast.

Tom had breakfast all prepared when the two officers came back downstairs, and they, —themselves, —completely nude and bare assed.

Tom and Jim watched as the two hot hunks came walking toward them, and Jim commented, "Damn man! Do those dicks keep getting longer and longer every day? Shit men, I swear half of your body weight is hanging down between your legs! Let's eat, —but guys, —you gotta sit at the table, and hide those logs, or I'm never gonna be able to eat and keep my eyes off of those sausages! Damn man, they look hotter today than they did last night!"

With smiles on everybody's faces, and joy in their hearts, they ate to their hearts content, and kept telling each other how excited they each were of the turn of events. Tom and Jim finally lost their concern that perhaps maybe they had done the wrong thing, and Jackson and Tyler got them convinced that it was definitely best this way! Surprising, yes! But best!

Jim looked at Officer Jackson and then Officer Tyler and said, "Tom and I have talked almost the whole night last night. We've got some stuff we want to see what you two think of. First, we were headed for Denver to visit our sister, but we did not tell her we were coming, so she's not expecting us. If we can, we'd like to stay here for a couple of days, maybe use the barn to sleep in, and just forget about going on to Denver."

"Hey Tyler, what do you think? I like that idea! Tyler, what do you say?" Officer Jackson gleefully asked.

"Yeah, I sure don't see any problem with that. It works for me! Sounds like fun, but you sure don't have to use the barn! You guys wanting to find out some more new stuff while you're here? I mean, like do more than just stay, but kind of play around some more, I assume?"

"Yeah, oh yeah! Yeah, that is what we mean!" Tom exclaimed.

"Yeah, that's what we mean. We're both kind of liking what is going on here, and neither one of us has ever had some big dicks like those two to play with, and we want to do more of it. If it's okay with you two, we'd like to stay."

"Sure, yeah, of course, sounds like fun to us!" Officer Jackson added.

"Then there is something else that we talked about too." Tom said.

Looking at both brothers, Officer Jackson then asked Tom, "Yeah, well, what is that?"

"We want to move here. Neither one of us like our jobs very well, neither one of us really like where we live, and since Mom and Dad are both gone, there is no reason for us to live there anymore. That was one of the reasons were going to go visit our sister. We thought that if she could pick up and move, then maybe we should do the same thing, but after getting to know you two, we decided last night that we'd like to move here, close to you guys, if you guys thought that might work for us. We'd never tell anybody of how we met you guys. That's only our business and nobody else's. We'd have to find someplace to live and find jobs, and we were kind of hoping that maybe you guys could help us do that. I work for a company doing scheduling and transportation planning, and Jim works in a sporting goods store, as an assistant manager. Do you guys think maybe we could find some jobs around here somewhere, kind of like those?"

"Hey Tyler, what do you think about that?" Jackson asked as he looked over toward his buddy. "How weird is that? Is there some kind of a special power taking over here or something?"

Tyler grinned, and looking at Jackson replied. "Man, this is way too weird! This is going way beyond us just finding their car in the drive. Jackson, is this some kind of a funny set up against me or something? I know you really owe me one for that mess I made out of your birthday party, but is this whole thing some kind of a get-back-at me? Are these two guys a total gag against me that I just haven't caught onto yet?"

"No Tyler, no! No Tyler this is for real man!"

Jim and Tom looked at the two officers and did not understand just what they were talking about or what Officer Tyler's confusion was all about.

"No Tyler, this is a complete shock to me too! Tyler, this is for real man!"

Then looking at the brothers, Officer Jackson continued. "I know you guys are all confused here. Tyler thinks this conversation is some kind of gag against him. He thinks I'm trying to get even with him of him hiring a gal stripper for my birthday party last year. No guys, he's all confused because of some comments we made while he was fucking my ass this morning. This is way too weird!"

Jim and Tom looked at Officer Jackson with very confused expressions on their faces.

"Guys, this morning while Tyler was fucking the hell out of my ass, we had a lot of, —what we thought was joking, conversations about how we should have tricked you two guys into staying here for awhile. We really went though some really wild things about how we could have made you guys stay around here for awhile, which, yes I will admit, one was having you kind of arrested, not for real, —but just kind of, so that you thought you had to stay. We really played with a lot of ideas of what we could have done, to make you think you had to say here for a few days. Hey, we had fun with you guys last night, and we were real pissed at ourselves that we had let you guys go! Or, so we thought so anyway! Now, —for you to tell us that you want to move here, that is great! Tyler, how in the hell does that sound to you? Sounds great to us, doesn't it? We'll get to fuck their asses with our big dicks all the time now!"

"Shit man! If this is really for real, it sure sounds great to me! Jackson, I don't really think the guys will need to find someplace to live, do you? You've got room here enough for one of them, and I sure can fix up that extra room in my house for the other one. Uh—guys. Do you guys live together now? I mean, if we did what I was thinking, one would live here and the other one at my place. Is that a problem? Would that work for you guys?"

"No, we don't live together. I'd say that is probably the real reason that until last night neither one of us ever got fucked by the other guy." Tom said. "No, we have separate places. Shit man! If we had been living together, then maybe I would have seen that big woody my big brother has, and then I would have been getting it before last night. But, Officer Tyler, which one of us would live where? I like the idea, but how do we decide who lives at which place?"

"Well, I don't know. I guess Jackson and I need to sit down and kind of decide that. Oh hey, Jackson! I haven't even asked you if this line of thinking is okay with you. I mean, in my excitement, I'm making plans for you that I haven't even asked if you want to do that or not."

"Oh Yeah Tyler, I like the idea! Man, is stuff moving fast here? First, we pick up a couple of hot looking asses, —in a fake stop, find out they are brothers, find out that they have never sucked or fucked each other yet, and then get to watch them take each other for the first time, wow! Then, to follow that, get up this morning and find out that they have secretly fixed us a good big breakfast, and in the bare, no less! Now the top glory is to find out that we are going to get to keep them! Tyler, I haven't felt like this since I was about six years old and got my first puppy! Shit man, this means that I'm gonna have one of 'em here at my house all of the time, and whenever I need it, I guess I'll have a hungry ass here, just waiting for me to get home, and pound it! Wow! Man! What a fucking night!"

Tyler looked at Jackson, grinned, then looked at Jim and Tom and asked, "Well guys, just how soon can you guys quit your jobs, clean out, whatever you have to do back home, and then get your asses back out here?"

Jim kind of looked at Tom in a rather asking, 'Am I right' mode, and said, "Well, I think once we get back home, we can turn in our two week notices, and during those two weeks get everything packed and get back here right after that. We both live in apartments, so we don't have to worry about selling houses or anything. When Mom and Dad got killed in the traffic accident, we sold the old family house so that Tammy, our sister, could get her part of the estate before she moved, so I think our getting out is going to go pretty smoothly, don't you Tom?"

"Yeah I agree. You know I kind of think that Jim and I have both had it in the back of our minds that we each knew the day would soon come when we would do something like this, so neither one of us got too tied down back there once the family place was sold. We just never had a real good reason to really talk about it until last night, after you guys left the barn and came in here. After it was just the two of us, we let each other know how much we each wanted to live close to you guys! Wow, I can't believe this. Is this really happening? I'm not drunk or crazy or dreaming or something, am I?"

"No Tom, you're not dreaming! This is real!" Officer Jackson said. "Now, we just need to figure out who is going to live with whom. Tom and me, or Jim and me, or which way? Hey wait a minute here! Wait one minute! Tom, you said you work for a company doing scheduling and transportation planning, right?"

"Yeah, yeah, I do that and Jim works in a sporting goods store as an assistant manager."

Jackson then looked over at Tyler and asked, "Well shit buddy! What in the hell have I been saying that I needed around here to help me get this barn thing going good and strong?"

Looking back at Jackson, and with a big shitty assed grin on his face, Tyler asked, "Oh shit man! Are you thinking what I think you are thinking? Hell yes man! Yeah, why not? Shit man that would work!"

Poor Tom and Jim just sat there in complete confusion. They each looked at each other, then at the other two men. Neither one said anything. They had no idea of what to say or what to ask.

"Tom, you will be living with me!" Officer Jackson said. "Tom I need a man here to head up the barn-rent business thing. I fixed that barn up to be rented out for events, and since I'm here so seldom, it's not getting the use that it should be, and if you will agree, I'd like for you to rather head up that business for me. By renting that out more often, we can make enough money to give you a full time job, you live here in my place, and after we really get it going real well, then I can make some money off of it too. Tom, what do you think?"

"Hey man! What can I say? Sure I like it. When I quit back home, I can tell them I already have a new job! And you want me to live here with you? Is that right?"

"Yeah, yeah that's what I mean. I've got the room for you, and you already know about the playroom out in the barn. You just might be a good addition out there too! Some of my buddies that stop by to use the playroom just might really like having you available for out there when I'm not home. Hey, some of them are some pretty hot built cops, too! You know how cops get themselves all frustrated and need a good strong firm ass to take their frustrations out on. A lot of them have found out that they can fuck some guy's ass good and hard, but they just can't fuck that way with their women, so they like having some guy available, for whenever they need it. With you here, then they can get into the playroom, and then maybe have some fun with you too, while they're here! What do you think? You game?"

"Yeah, I like it! I like it a lot! Jim, what do you think? Is this all okay with you? I mean, I don't want to do stuff that you don't think I should do? What do you think?"

"What can I say? Hell yes, I think that sounds like one hell of an idea. I mean the job. The other fucking around stuff, well if that was me, I'd be all excited about it, but since it's you, I do have to remember that I am your big brother, and act like it's not such a good idea."

Then Jim reached over, rubbed his brother on the head, and said, "Hell yes guy! Go for it! Shit man, maybe I can just happen to be out here once in awhile too! Now if I can find me a job as quickly and as easily, things will be good."

Officer Tyler looked at Jim, and asked, "Jim, what do you think about working for a company that sells uniforms? Like you know, officer's uniforms and that kind of stuff? Direct sales to the customer. In a store."

"Shit yes! Hell yes!" Jim replied. "Do you know someplace that needs some help?"

"Yeah, I do." Officer Tyler replied. "We get our stuff at a company called "All Dressed Right, Uniforms and Equipment" and I know the guy that owns it. It's Jake Campbell. When I was in the store last Tuesday he told me that one of his salesmen was moving to the west coast and that he was going to be short of help. Hell at the time, I didn't think anything about it, but I guess that is why we tell other people stuff that is going on in our lives. Jim, if you think that might be a fit for you, I'll give Jake a call and find out if he has, by any funny chance, found someone within the last two or three days. I know damn well he hasn't though. I know Jake well enough to know he'd rather find employees through friends rather than put an ad in the newspaper."

"Hell yes I think that would be good. I've got a lot of sales experience. Yeah, but hey, —will I be able to help the customers try on their uniforms?" Jim asked with a laugh in his voice.

"Hey, horny guy, let's get you the job first, then you can see if you can tuck everything down in for those guys or not."

Tyler got up from the table, had some phone conversation, then turned toward Jim and asked, "Hey Jim, can you go talk to Jake, Monday morning at about ten?"

"Yeah, yes! Of course I can!" Jim quickly answered. Shit man, I can not believe this! Shit man! God, I can't believe how fast everything is happening! Tom, we are actually going to move here! All that stuff we talked about last night, it's really happening! And it's working better than we thought it would."

Officer Tyler finished talking to Jake, returned to the table and told the others, "Jake is real happy that I called. He told me that he knew that if he mentioned that to enough of the officers, one of us would come up with somebody. Then he very quietly asked, if I knew this guy up real close. He knows my ways. He and I have done some playing around before, so anyway Jim, he already knows you are gay. I hope that is okay. Any problem with that?"

"No, no, —I really don't care. That's what I am, and I'm just glad that others accept it when they find out. So, I guess that means Jake is gay too?"

"Oh no! Did not mean to imply that!" Officer Tyler quickly exclaimed. "No! I should not have implied that! Jake is a married guy with a couple of kids, but he has had reason to have me back in the shop late at night, usually for a special fitting, and you know what will happen when two guys get together in a back room, kind of late at night, and one of them happens to like dick."

"Oh, so you were having your uniform pants fitted? You had your pants off, I assume? What did he do, feel you up or something?" Jim asked.

"Well yeah, but that's not the reason we did our thing. We got to kind of joking around, and when he reached up in my crotch to hold the tape measure, I made some jokes about doing that to him, and from that point on, it was all a grab ass and crotch session. I finally got him down, de-pantsed him, and got his rod out. I had to pin him to the floor though! I sucked him off, but he didn't do me. But hey, that was fine with me. I had my fun, and I guess he must have liked it. He actually told me to do it to him again, another night, when we were alone. So anyway, don't mention that to him. Okay? Hey, if you do, I'm afraid he might not hire you since you already know too much! Okay?"

"Yeah, okay! No, I'd never mention something like that. But it is nice to know that he will already know about me, so that I don't feel like I need to hide stuff. But, I definitely will not let him know that he got sucked off! Uhh, —Officer Tyler. Does this mean that I will get to rent your extra room?"

"Shit yes! Hell yes! Well, anyway we'll call it renting my extra room, but gotta be honest about it man, I doubt that you'll be sleeping in that room very often! I'm gonna have me a man at home too, just waiting for me to come home and pound the hell out of his ass, — right?"

"Oh shit yes man, hell yes!" Jim almost yelled with excitement! "Yeah, every night man, —every night!"

"Hey men, this is working out way too damn good! If it's going to take you guys about two weeks to get back here, from whenever you get home, that'll give me enough time to get that room all painted and ready for you. What color do you want me to paint it? Cum shot white? Maybe we can paint your walls so they match my chest! With you in the house, I expect a lot of stuff to turn, —cum shot white!"

Sitting there with a major grin on his face, Jim looked at his brother Tom, then at Officer Tyler, and finally at Officer Jackson and said, "Never in the entire time of the world, could anybody ever believe that getting pulled over, by a Highway Patrolman, one hell of a fucking hot and fucking built Highway Patrolman, and then, him hearing me almost yell, about how hot his uniform pants were kissing his ass, could ever turn out this good! Thanks man, thanks! Give me my ticket officer, —give me my ticket! Put it in my butt!"

BRAD'S EARLY MORNING WALK HOME

CHAPTER ONE:

Why Is He Unbuttoning My Shorts?

At ten minutes till two in the morning, Brad did not care for the situation that he had now found himself in, and he definitely did not care for the neighborhood that he was walking through. He knew that he was not exactly the, 'go to Sunday School' type of a guy, and for the gays that hung out in that part of town, yes, he was pretty well known as the slut of the city. But, getting mugged and probably torn up by having stuff like baseball bats rammed in your ass, was not his way of enjoying an evening out! True, he's had his ass used a hell of a lot more than just once this evening, but still and yet, he knew that he'd still like to have it usable for future fuckings, —and not have to beg off of getting it up in the ass, since some group of hoodlums had grabbed him, and forced something like a yard rake or a fire-hose nozzle up in him.

The city bus system shuts down at 1 AM each night, and enjoying the evening at the Bum Rap gay bar, as he did, Brad had failed to leave in time to catch a bus, so his only choice now was to walk home.

Dressed in a pair of short cut off jeans, a ripped and torn T-shirt, and sandals, Brad was not at all pleased with the aspect of having to walk through this particular section of town, especially looking a little too much like some available, gay hustler, type of guy. Right then, he was wishing he did not look quite so, "hot."

As he walked, he maintained a strong awareness of his surroundings and attempted to be aware of anybody or anything around him. He knew this section of town was not the 'friendly family' type of neighborhood. Way too many news articles out of this area, and he still had about five more blocks to walk before he felt like his life and safety were not in so much danger. He loved to have his ass played with, but not by a group of guys that wouldn't even call the emergency crew is everything got way out of hand and, —let's say, 'all torn up!'

As he kept a quick and steady pace, he realized that he could hear an automobile behind him, and he was very aware, that automobile was not moving any faster than he was walking. Keeping his eyes forward, he did not turn to look, knowing that if he did, that would be the beginning of big, deep trouble for him, due to the type of hoodlums that control this area.

As Brad continued to walk, he continued to hear that car behind himself. He was very uncomfortable, and not exactly feeling very safe. As he approached a small, old and very unkempt city park, he heard the automobile speed up as if to catch up to him. He continued his steady pace until he heard, from the external speaker on the car, "Put your hands in the air, face the park and do not turn around."

"Oh shit!" Brad thought. "Shit man, I don't know what in the hell I did, but at least it is a cop and not some thugs!"

Brad put his hands in the air, faced the park and heard the patrol car door open, and he could then hear the police radio from inside of the cruiser. Then he heard two car doors close. Two officers! He did not realize that two officers were there.

Brad heard instructions. "Keep your hands in the air, and walk into the park. Go over there, toward that little grassy area!"

Having no idea at all as to just what was happening, but feeling better about the fact that these were city policemen, and not gun-toting thugs, Brad did as he was instructed. He simply knew that if that car had turned out to be some "bad ass rough guys," that his whole existence would have been in shear danger, and if he did manage to live though the rest of the night, he would probably be ripped and torn from getting fucked and mouth cock rammed, as roughly as they could do him. He simply knew that those types of actions do happen, in this section of town, and way too often! Troubled, and confused, —at least Brad knew he was safe from danger. Officers and, thank God, not rough thugs that could, and probably would, rip his whole body apart, all the way from his asshole to his mouth, just having their fun with it. He knew that to some of the guys around these parts, the safety of a guy was not so important, —what was more important was, —how much fun could they have with another person's body?

Brad was given additional instructions as he approached the more grassy area. "Keep you hands up and grab ahold of that tree branch. Do not turn around, nor look around. Do not look at us!"

"Wow!" Brad thought. "How weird!" But having never been arrested before, or whatever this was, that was happening, he was going to follow orders, to the order.

Brad grabbed the branch that he was instructed to get ahold of, and as he did, he felt one of the officers reach around him, and unbutton his cut-offs. "What in the world?" Brad questioned to himself. "What is going on? What is he doing? Why is he unbuttoning my shorts?"

The officer then pulled Brad's cut-offs and his jock strap down, and told him to lay down on the grass and keep his face hidden on the ground.

As Brad did what he was instructed, he heard the sound of the officers sturdy leather belt and it's buckle, plus the sound of his uniform zipper being pulled down. Almost immediately, and without any type of announcement, Brad was getting his ass fucked to its fullest extent, by, what must have been a very, very large cock, firmly sticking out from in front of his now, apparent, "officer fuck buddy."

Suddenly without any type of warning, the officer flopped himself down on Brad's back and without hesitation or apparently even needing to aim it, he rammed his human officer's shaft into the deepest of Brad's ass. The officer did not have, or at least did not express, any concerns about if Brad was used to getting big dicks rammed up in there. Fit or not, that dick was going in, and going in all the way! It did! No fanfare. No grabbing the cheeks of the ass and pulling them apart. No finger in the hole first! No checking the ass to see if it was slippery or not! And definitely no asking the guy that owned the asshole if he wanted it, or was ready for it. Just one big push, and one small squeal from Brad, and one rather long drawn out moan of complete pleasure from the fucking officer, as he pushed his policeman's cock into Brad's asshole, as far as he could plant it, and then try for even more depth, after he had gone as far as possible.

As Brad accepted the shock of what was happening to him, definitely all of a sudden, and without warning, (and by a person that he thought was his protector, his protector that would protect him from anything similar to this, of happening), he realized that he was having his head pulled up high enough so that his mouth would fit nicely onto the eight or nine inch, thick cock that was now being rather quickly placed into his mouth. The other officer, without saying anything at all, had dropped his uniform pants, had knelt down in front of Brad's face, and was now fucking, and completely filling, Brad's mouth. The officer had ahold of Brad's head, and was using Brad's head and mouth to jerk himself off with. All the officer said was, "Oh man, this is so much better than using my hand!"

Brad was in complete shock of what was happening. Shock and pleasure! Shock that all of this was happening without so much as a "Do you want to get fucked" question, and pleasure knowing that he was getting fucked, one on each end of his body, by two of the 'city's finest'.

As the officer that was fucking his butt hole pumped, —with all of his might and strength, Brad knew that he was just about to get it from a city policeman, and never in his life had he ever thought that "getting it from a city employee" would ever be so exciting, so fulfilling and so warm at the same time. He knew that at any moment his ass was going to be used as the hungry receptacle for the officer's cum shot, or shots. As they hit, Brad realized that using the plural was the correct. Shot one hit, then shot two hit, and it felt even stronger and more forceful than shot one had, and then number three hit! Brad wondered to himself just how long it had been since this ass fucking officer, had shot off. Brad's ass felt like it had been completely filled to the brim, with police officer cum.

Brad's mental thoughts were, "What a load! What a feeling! Oh man! I felt him shoot in me at least three times! This is great! What a great very unexpected thing to have happen! Shit man, I want to know who these officers are. I want to do this again, and again. Damn man, they are so damn hot! Damn man! They are using me just the way I love to be used and I don't know if they know that or not, or if I just happened to be one lucky stiff, tonight! Damn, I wonder if they know something about me or not. I wonder if I'm just their latest toy on the street guy? Man, I have to find out some way who these two guys are. Man, I like what they are doing to me, and I like how they are doing it!"

Just as Brad was celebrating the sweet success, and the great feelings that were happening back in his tight little asshole, he realized that his head was being held very tightly and being pulled into the crotch of his face fucking officer, and he heard the officer rather groan. "Oh man! Oh shit man! I hope you can swallow cum while you get your mouth rammed full! Oh shit man, I'm cumming! I'm cumming!"

As he was saying, "I'm cumming, I'm cumming," the officer pulled Brad's head closer and closer to his crotch, to the point where Brad could only slightly breathe. His entire face was buried in the crotch fuzz of his, unknown, but hot, and very well hung, mouth fucking, police officer.

Brad did not really need to be told that the officer was cumming. He was very well aware of that as he tried to swallow as quickly as he could, and then clamp down on that stick for another load and swallow it as quickly as he could, again. "Shit, oh shit!" He thought to himself. "At least three shots in the ass, and now at least that many down my throat! Shit man! I have just been loaded with at least six cum shots from our city's finest. And regardless of how many other officers there are out there, right now these two truly are the city's finest! I know! I am the only one in town right now that really knows how damn fine, hot and drained, these two men are!"

As officer number one pulled his dripping, but still very strong and stiff cock out of Brad's ass, officer number two did the same from Brad's mouth, but not before wiping the extra, spill out, cum off of Brad's face with the end of his cock.

Office number one, told Brad, "OK man! Get up, and keep looking the other way, don't look at us, and get yourself all put back together so you can get back onto your way home.

Both officers stood behind Brad and rather repaired themselves into the respectful appearance that the city officers are expected to present. — not the very recent, 'Officer with pants down, hard-on sticking out, and cum dripping from the meaty head of his shaft."

As Brad pulled his jock strap and his cut-offs up and covered his very, very happy ass, he heard, who he could only refer to as officer #1, say, "OK get yourself all presentable, and head for the sidewalk. Do not look back at us! We will be following you in the cruiser, far enough to make sure you are out of this nasty, trashy, fucking part of town and to make sure you are safe, before we go our own way. Next Wednesday morning, same time, same place! Understand? But have a little more grease left up in your butt than you had tonight. Next week you get his dick, and you are going to need more grease up in there if you want to enjoy it, like I do. Now walk! And, do not look back! Understand?"

Brad very happily replied, "Yes Sir, I do understand. Walk! Do not look back! One week from now! One week from tonight! Same place, but more grease! Yes Sir! I do understand!"

Brad turned, walked toward the street, and internally, and mentally celebrated that, "Only one week to go! Only one week!"

CHAPTER TWO:

Yes, He Did Have Some Grease Left Up In There

All day long, for that entire Tuesday, the only thing that Brad could think about was the very firm instructions that he had heard, late at night, the week earlier, when the officer told him, —did not ask him, mind you, —but rather very firmly and very strongly told him, "Next Wednesday morning, same time, same place!"

Brad's anxiety had been growing and growing as the day moved along. He knew that he simply had to be at that old park at, or very close to a quarter till two in the morning, and he definitely remembered that he had been instructed to, "have a little more grease left up in your butt!" That comment, and instruction, definitely left him wondering just how did that officer know for sure that he already had some grease up in there, or had he just slammed his cock up in his ass, just taking a chance that his ass was either loose enough that his thick cock would go in, and to its entire length, —without any problem, —or did he actually know there would be some grease left in there, and from —what prior activity?

As Brad had continued his walk home the prior week, and after the rough ass fucking and face fucking that he had enjoyed, that question continued to surface again and again. The very straight forward instruction to have a little more grease left up in there, was a very confusing, straight forward, statement. Yes, he did, in-fact, have some grease left up in there, but how in the world could that officer have known that? Or did he just assume that?

Tonight was going to be a very similar night for Brad as he had lived the Tuesday evening, 7 days earlier, with one exception. Tonight, just before he leaves the Bum Rap bar, he will be going into the restroom and pushing a good amount of grease up into his ass, so that it will be obvious that he had followed instructions.

The Bum Rap bar had what was "supposed" to be a very secret and unknown basement room, but it did seem that more and more guys were happening to find out about it, and using that room to their advantage, while at the bar. It is because of that basement room that, the week earlier, Brad was still carrying some grease up in his ass.

The basement room was actually a storage room and a utility room, but if you "just happened to know", where the door to the basement stairs was located, then you also knew that it was never locked. To know where the door was at, you had to know the very confusing path around boxes and the extra chairs and tables, stored upstairs. Very convenient placement of the extra equipment provided just the right amount of shelter for the 'unknown', and 'non-existent' door.

On any given night, especially after about 11 PM, the storage room would be very crowded and every man down there was either getting or giving whatever his personal desire was. Brad's ass was a rather well known, no— a 'very well known', element of the basement. He spent so much time down there, totally naked, face and hands up against the wall, leaning against the wall as if to be making love to it, and his ass standing out proud and available, that some of his closer friends, and some of his more anxious fuckers would bring drinks down to the basement for him. His ass was such a sweet treat, to so many guys, that they did not want him to have any necessity of going upstairs, to get himself a drink. They were way too concerned that they might loose their turn in line, their turn for using his ass, as their own personal cum depository, if he disappeared for a few minutes, to grab himself a drink. In-fact, upstairs, all you needed to do was tell the bartender what you personally wanted, and then tell him, "Brad too," and he would automatically fix Brad's preferred Bourbon and coke. The bar knew of Brad's popularity in the basement, and they were also smart enough to realize that Brad's attendance was a business boom for them. Any night that Brad was there, the base of customers stayed longer than on other nights, and that they poured many more drinks, on those, "Brad", nights. Brad had become rather an attraction feature of, 'why to go to the Bum Rap', although none of this had been planned.

One night about three or four weeks earlier, one of Brad's friends had asked him how many times he had been fucked, on that particular night, while down in the basement, and Brad had to admit that he really did not know. He told his friend that he knew there was actually a line forming back behind him, and just as quickly as one cock was pulled out, he was taking another one, and how many, and who they were, he did not have any idea. Hey, —yeah, he admitted, he had experienced one great time, but the "who and the how many", he did not know. He admitted, that for a short while, that night, he truly did feel like some male whore, but the excitement of what was happening to him and his ass, was so great, that he just let the negative feelings pass, and he concentrated on what was happening to his ass and how great it was feeling. He did tell his friend that he had taken one cock up in his ass that he truly did wish he had found out who it belonged to. He told his buddy, that particular cock felt so much bigger than any other cock he had ever ass-eaten before, and how, now, he was wishing he knew who the guy was, so that he could ask for it again. He was really pissed at himself that he had not turned and looked to see who was fucking him at that time. Shaking his head, he had told his buddy that to try and guess as closely as he could, he thought maybe he had been fucked probably 12 to 15 times, but he did not know if some of them were what he could call, "repeat business," or not. He just knew, that the guy with the really oversized cock had only screwed him once. He knew that, after he had gotten rammed with that pole the first time, he just kept hoping for it again, but it never stuck, again!

It was this action, in the basement, that had provided the grease that Brad was still toting around, the week before. But, he kept pondering the question, —how in the world did that officer know that he already has some grease up in there, and know to tell him to "have a little more grease left up in there," the following week. The wording, "left up in there," was what had him so confused. Was there some way that officer could have known that his ass had already been fucked that night, or was that officer just assuming that? Brad could not decide which way to think. He felt that if that office had just assumed that Brad had some grease up in there, then he was a very gutsy guy, in just ramming his asshole, as fast and as hard, as he had, without first finding out for sure, and if he did know there was grease up in there, how in the world did he know?

Brad had come to the bar just a little later than usual, and some of his usual Tuesday night friends had become nervous that he was going to be a no show for some reason.

"No, No!" He explained. "No, I know I'm a little late, but I just needed some extra time to myself before I came in tonight, but hey guys, —I'm here now!"

Brad ordered himself his usual Bourbon and coke, and as he retreated over toward the bottle shelf, along the wall, his friend, and one of his usual fuckers, Sam, approached.

"Hey Brad my man! How you doing?" Sam asked. "I was getting a little nervous thinking that maybe I was going to have to go without or find myself getting very lucky someplace else, when you weren't here earlier. What's up man?"

Brad greeted Sam and told him he was real glad he was there and waiting on him. "Hey Sam, I really need you and just about as quickly as we can sneak down to the basement. Seen anybody in here tonight that we need to keep the door hidden from?"

"Yeah." Sam answered. "There's a couple of two or three guys sitting up at the front end of the bar that I don't know, so when we go down, we've got to be real cool about it. I've never seen them in here before. Why don't you head that way, and I'll follow you very shortly. OK?"

"Yeah, OK," Brad said. "I'll be down there and you'll find me over by the old furnace. Don't take too long, my ass is real anxious, and when you get down there, I'll tell you why."

Brad turned and casually walked toward the back or the bar and finally disappeared down the stairs to the basement. He quickly shed everything that he had on, —a firm, tit fitting, and showing, tank top, —a pair of cut-offs, —a pair of very, very skin tight, short and really sexy biker shorts, —and of course his sandals. Brad grabbed his small plastic container of grease and applied a fair amount up into his ass. Being as anxious, as he was right then for some ass action, he not only inserted the grease, but he continued to finger himself, and with closing his eyes and throwing his head back, he made believe, to himself, that his own finger was actually the cock hanging on that police officer, that he knew he was going to be getting in just about four hours. He had been anxious for this night for a whole week now, and the time was now getting short.

As he was fingering his own as hole, he had a terrible thought of "Oh shit! What if those officers get all tied up doing some real business and they can't come meet me at the park? Oh shit!" He thought. "Crap! I haven't thought of that happening all week. Oh shit man! What if something goes wrong?"

As he was pondering his worrying thoughts, and at the same time feeling the interior of his own asshole, Sam came down the stairs, carrying not only his own drink, but a new fresh one for Brad.

"OK man!" Sam said. "So what is going on that you are so damn anxious for my rod tonight. What's happening?"

"Sam," Brad answered. "Sam, I am so damn horny tonight. I've got two policemen that fucked me last week, and I was told to meet them at the same place, same time, tonight, and man, just me getting it in both ends from them at the same time, and especially in such a dangerous, trashy, public place, has really got me all hot and bothered. The officers are hot, both of them, but you know man, I've never been fucked out in the open like that before, and when it happened last week, I really did not think too much about it being in the public view, if anybody happened to look, but remembering it this week, has got me all excited and breathing real heavy! I need to get a cock up in my ass to try and get me calmed back down. As this day moved on, I have just gotten myself all worked up with just the idea of knowing, one policeman in my ass, and another policeman in my mouth, and all three of us doing it out in a public place where anybody could walk up on us. Damn man, —I am so damn anxious! I want to get it going, and I want to get it going, right now! Sam I did not know, that the idea of me getting my ass fucked out in a public place like that was such a turn on to me! I've never been fucked in a public park before, and last week I wasn't thinking too much about where I was, it was more about who I was getting fucked by, but Sam! God! The idea of getting fucked out in a public park is really exciting! Shit man! I wonder if I will ever be happy just getting fucked in a private room anymore. And, two cops! Public park, and two cops in me? Oh man! Shit Sam! I am so damn anxious to do it again!"

Sam put the drinks down, and immediately undressed and let his 8" stiff uncut cock fly. "Brad, give me you ass, and after I get my cock all slid up in you, you start telling me just what in the hell happened last week, and what is supposed to be going on tonight. You have got me so damn hot now that I have to hear every little minute detail of everything that is happening. Hang on man, I am about to ram your anxious, hungry, horny, public anxious, asshole. Don't move, here I come!"

Sam turned Brad around to face the wall and immediately rammed his man meat, beef steak rod, up into Brad's rear end. Brad's body was slammed against the wall as Sam's cock entered his asshole and Sam then slammed into him. Sam's body pushed Brad forward as he lunged toward Brad, and drove his rod in as deeply as it could possibly go.

Hugging the wall with his arms and hands extended upward, was Brad's favorite position when in the basement, for giving his ass, to whoever happened to be the "man of the minute" at that specific time. Any dick, any man, —neither was of any concern to Mr. ass-hungry Brad! Brad's only concern was, being in the basement and not having some guy's cock rammed up in his ass. His attitude was, "If I'm in the basement, then I need a dick up in my ass the whole time! That's why I am down there!"

As Sam fucked Brad, Brad attempted to tell Sam what had happened the prior week, and attempted to tell him what he expected to have happen, yet that night. With Sam ramming Brad's ass, and ramming much more forcefully as each of Brad's explanations got more exciting, Brad did have some trouble attempting to continue the talking. Once in awhile, Brad would have to just simply quit, so that he could let out a small confined squeal, the result of the strong and forceful motion of being rammed up inside of his ass. It was confusing to determine if his excitement was, (1) it was from the ass fucking that he was currently getting, or (2) from the thoughts about the two policemen fucking him, that he knew he was scheduled to be getting a little later.

As the evening moved on, more participants visited the basement, and each man had his own personal desires of exactly why he was in the basement, and no short number of them were there to get their weekly piece of Brad's ass. Brad had asked Sam to not discuss his, later in the night, situation with anyone, since he wanted to be sure everything worked out OK, before anybody else knew about the double fucking he was getting from the policemen.

Brad did not consider himself a male-whore, but if a person were to figure out the exact amount of money that Brad did not need to spend on his evening of drinking, it could easily be said that Brad was, in-fact, getting paid for being the available and tight asshole in the basement. Brad was in the basement for more than three hours, almost constantly with a dick of someone's up in his ass, and during that entire time he had no reason to go upstairs to get himself a drink. In-fact, after having about six or eight of the complementary ones given to him, all purchased by his anxious tops, Brad knew that he had to quit drinking or he was going to be one plain ole street drunk, as he attempted to get to his, now "favored and preferred," city park.

"Sam, I need to go upstairs and maybe get myself some coffee." He told Sam. Sam had been his kind of "man in attendance" while in the basement. Brad had not asked him to stay there, but Sam simply knew that Brad often allowed himself to get just a little too much ass fucking, and along with it, a little too much alcohol. So he rather felt the necessity of hanging around to make sure that nothing too rough, got going on, that Brad, with a little too much alcohol in him, could not take care of. Sam knew that Brad just got way too horny and way too excited, to protect himself.

The night that Brad had allowed himself to be fist fucked, —for his very first time, was the night that Sam decided that Brad really needed a friend to stand by, just incase somebody got too rough. The fist fucking turned out OK, in-fact, it showed Brad another excitement in sex that he had not yet experienced, but to Sam, the way he had been "talked into" getting fisted, was a little too alarming. He felt that the fister was not really giving Brad a chance to say "No", —if he had wanted to. Obviously, Brad did not wish to say, No! Later, Brad realized that he was very glad that he had not refused it, and that he had accepted the man's challenge to take it. Brad's thinking concept was, —if a dick can feel that good up in there, then just think of what a big fist will feel like. He took it, and he loved it! That, of course, turned out to be only the first time, of getting a fist up in his ass.

On this particular night, Brad was glad he had Sam around as his buddy and acting kind of like his 'bodyguard'. Brad knew that with his excitement and anxiety for the, 'yet to happen events of the evening', he was not keeping himself under too much control. He knew that he always had a very available asshole and a very hungry asshole, (and he also knew that any top that had ever been in that bar in the last few years, had probably, at one time or another, been in it) but tonight he just knew that he was wanting it played with so roughly and so forcefully that he probably was letting himself get a little out of control, and was letting guys treat him much more dangerously and roughly than normal. He did remember being body slammed up against the wall by a couple of guys during the evening. Guys that were really taking advantage of his anxious and very hungry, "do me men," attitude. In-fact, he could remember one guy earlier in the evening making a remark to him, something to the fashion about how damn horny Brad was acting that night! It did not come across to that fucker that anything was wrong. He was simply expressing how excited that was getting him, and that he hoped that Brad would stay that way for future sessions. He liked the more rough actions that Brad was encouraging the men to take with him and with his ass. He liked the way Brad was begging to be used and abused. He made a comment just before he pulled his cock out, that he had never, in his entire fucking "career," ever had a guy that begged for, —more!, —harder!, —deeper!, as much as Brad was doing that night.

Brad and Sam rather closed up the basement action for the night, and within only minutes of their return to the bar upstairs, the basement had become empty. All of a sudden the actual bar had become crowded again. Only a few minutes earlier, it looked like the bar was not really doing very much business.

The only concern the bar owners had about this occurrence, happening at their bar, was to maintain its secrecy so that the law did not shut them down.

So far, and actually for a number of years now, everything had been going OK, and they had not received any city problems, even though every once in awhile they would have a couple of policemen stop in during the day, as if to just look around. The bartender would always offer them a coke and let them spend as much time visiting as they wished, then they would wonder on. Couple of months later, either the same two, or another two, would stop back in, have their coke, have some conversation, look around, and then be gone. After each visit, the on duty bartender, and any "aware" customers would take a sigh of relief, take a deep breath and then 'comment' (with a grin on their faces) on how glad they were that the officers felt comfortable visiting a gay bar once in awhile.

Sam and Brad positioned themselves in a corner table where they had some privacy, and rather contemplated Brad's planned moves for the rest of the evening.

"Well, last week I got to the park right at about ten minutes till two. I left here right at about 1:30, so I guess the walk there took me about 20 minutes. I want to be in the area just a few minutes earlier tonight so they know I'm showing up, so I think I will leave here right at about 20 or 25 minutes after. What time is it right now?" Brad asked Sam.

"It's right at ten minutes after one." Sam replied. "Now Brad, do you feel safe doing this tonight, or do you want me to kind of trail you and keep you in my sight? I can follow you, but stay back far enough that nobody knows that I am there."

"No, no!" Brad exclaimed! "No! I'm afraid that if they saw you, they'd never stop at the park. Sam, these are police officers, they are screwing some guy out in the middle of a city park, you know damn well that they are going to be damn careful that nobody knows what they are up to. Yeah, I'm not so crazy about the walk through some of that part of town, but tonight I guess I've got a couple of cops that will be following me from some point, so I'm sure I will be OK. Hey, I'll be right back. I've got to go to the restroom and stuff some more grease up in my ass. I want it to be real obvious that I remembered their instructions. I'll be right back."

Brad left the table, went to the men's room and used one of the stalls so that the other guys using the restroom right then, did not ask him why he was cramming grease up in his ass, and then pulling his shorts back up. He did not want to have to do any explaining to anybody. He did not want this meeting messed up by anybody.

As he got back to the table, Brad asked Sam if he would take his cut-offs with him. "I'm just going to wear these bike shorts, and don't want to bother with the cut-offs."

Sam looked at him and told him. "Well man, all I can say right now is that I hope you make it all the way to the park. With that pair of Spandex or wherever that fabric is, you sure are showing everything to everybody, and walking down the street looking like that is just plain asking for somebody, anybody, to grab you off of the street and rape you. Are you sure you feel comfortable walking down the street showing that much? Your dick shows in them shorts as if you just simply had it painted."

"Yeah, I'm OK Sam. It's late. Most of the way it's kind of dark, and I want to look as hot for those two cops as I can. I want them to get really horny when they pull up behind me, if that's what they intend to do again like last week. Sam, I want them to really fuck my ass, and I want both of them tonight if I can. I figure wearing these bike pants is the closest thing I can do to actually walking down the street with my bare ass hanging out, and if I could get away with that tonight, I'd be doing it! When they drive up behind me, I'd really like to be showing them a bare ass! I want them hungry!"

"OK then, man. I just hope everything is OK and you are safe. Keep your eyes open and know what is going on around you till you get hooked up with those cops. Are you not wearing a shirt either? You are going bare-chested? Shit man! You really are anxious to show everything to everybody, aren't you? Damn man! I hope those cops think you are as hot looking as I do right now. Shit man, I'm ready to throw you across this damn table and let you have it up the ass again right here and now! You are looking good man! Go get 'em, man! Call me when you get home! I'm anxious to hear the details! I'll be waiting up for the call! OK?"

"Yeah, I will Sam, but I'm not sure what time it will be! It will be late, I hope anyway! OK, man. I'm on my way. Talk to you later. Pray for me that my cops don't stand me up! Later, man. Bye!"

CHAPTER THREE:

You Guys Found the Right one!

Brad left the bar and started his much anticipated walk. The walk that he had been thinking about all week long.

The street was pretty well empty, with the occasional, and exceptional car load of, what Brad had to assume were, other gays on their way home or to another party. Within the first 10 minutes on the street, there had been two automobiles that had passed Brad from behind, and with everybody in the car gawking at him, they then turned the next corner, went around the block, and drove up behind him again. The first car had two guys, and two gals in it.

"Peculiar seating," Brad thought as he saw them the first time. Both guys in the front, and both gals in the back seat. As they drove past the second time, Brad understood the seating arrangement a little better. Both guys yelled sexy comments to him about his hot tight ass, and the girls just looked. His hot ass, he decided, was not getting those gals excited. They were obviously much more interested in each other, than his bubble butt showing through those tight, slick, glossy, biker shorts. And his bulging crotch was of no interest to them either, although the guy in the driver's seat must have liked it, since he yelled out, "Hey Bud, show me what you've got hidden in there!"

The guy on the passenger side threw a paper out of the window as he yelled, "I want to fuck that ass," but Brad did not pick it up. He could only assume it was either a phone number or an address. Brad felt that ignoring it was the safer thing for him to do, although he really did wish that somebody else was around that could retrieve it for him. From what he could see, the guy on the passenger side looked pretty hot to him, and obviously was not too timid of a guy. Brad thought, "Hell he might be a good, long and strong fucker. I might be passing up the wrong thing here!"

The second car that drove around the block and then came back, had two guys in it. As they approached the second time, they slowed way down, and both guys looked and smiled, but neither of them made any comments. Brad's reaction was a little more frustrated with this car and its occupants. He could not decide if it was because he felt kind of a put-down that they did not make comments to him, or if it was their athletic, muscular arms that he could see, and wanted to be able to get his hands on and grab ahold of, so badly. He did decide that perhaps it was better that they did not offer him a ride, —they would have been very hard to turn down.

Brad realized that, "Whoa, man. I've been dreaming of my hooking-up with the two cops all week, so don't go and get yourself all excited over two other guys that you don't know anything about, and then blow your "two cops in the park" meeting. Hot, yeah, real hot, but they could be gay bashers too. Just because they happen to be built like all gay guys should be, does not mean that once you are within arms reach of them, that you are then going to be able to grab ahold of anything interesting. Brad watched the car slowly drive on as the passenger turned to take a final look, and Brad could only hope that his "package" was showing as nicely as he could show it. He was rather proud of his ability to show off a good sized package whenever he had extra tight pants or shorts on, and tonight he was wanting all of it to show like a grand prize winner!

As Brad continued his walk, he realized that he was now getting very close to the spot where just one week earlier he first heard the car slowly drive up behind him. He listened intently. He did not hear anything. He continued his walk, and as he did, continued to keep a very open ear, and a prayer in his mind that he would not be stood up.

Just as he caught the first sight of the park that he was so anxiously looking forward to, he did hear an automobile slowly coming up behind him. Knowing the type of neighborhood that he was in, he did not feel totally comfortable of not knowing for sure if it was the police car or not. Especially, since the way he was dressed! He knew that if the wrong type of guys drove up behind him, they would make mince meat out of him as they played with their "fag guy." If it was not the police car, he could be allowing himself to be put in a very grave danger. The actions that he had known about happening around this section of town were not exactly what he had any desire to be involved in. Especially, since he would be a victim, and not just some type of a play partner. Some of the "residents" of this neighborhood simply do not like gay guys. He continued to walk, and was very disappointed that there were no un-boarded building windows that he could attempt a glimpse of a reflection, to see what kind of a car was behind him.

As he continued closer and closer to the entrance of the park, he continued to wonder if he was going to be putting his life in danger if: (1) He turned and entered the park, and (2) if, that was not the police car behind him. "Knowing this area, I could be walking right toward my own grave and not know it," he told himself.

Just as he hit the point when he had to decide if to turn into the park or not, he heard a man rather yell, "Brad, walk into the park."

"Brad, walk into the park? Those cops don't know my name! I never told them my name! Who in the hell is this?" he pondered.

The confusion became a little too much for him, and he started to turn and look back at the man.

"Don't look at us! Keep walking into the park. This is week number two man!" The man from in the car, yelled toward Brad.

The phrase, 'Don't look at us' and the, 'Week number two' were rather comforting words for Brad to hear. The, 'Don't look at us' was exactly what he had been told last week, and the 'week number two' definitely let him know it was one of the two cops from last week.

The automobile followed him as Brad continued to walk into the park, and as it entered the park, the driver turned off its lights. He was now walking in front of the police cruiser with only the moon light available to see with. He knew the automobile was following him very closely, and as he would come to a new "intersection" in the park, he knew he was being told which path to take by the indication of the automobile turn signals. As he approached a split in the road, —well actually an old single lane path, the car's turn signal would either flash left or right. As he obeyed the instructions of the turn signal, he could faintly hear the car occupant says, "Good Boy!"

They had gone into the park much more deeply than where they had stopped last week. He had passed his tree, —where last week he was told to grab ahold and don't look back. Brad was hoping that this deeper area of the park actually meant a rougher and more time consuming session than what he had enjoyed the previous week. "I think they must be hiding their car back in here," he told himself. "Maybe they want more ass and more time tonight!"

Going deeper into the park was rather somewhat of a disappointment to Brad, since he remembered how exciting it had been last week to be so easily available, to be seen, by any person that just might happen upon them, but then at the same time, he was deeply hoping that his policemen fuckers were looking for a more extended stay this week than what had happened the prior week. He decided that he would gladly give up the rather public exposure for a longer fucking session. Last week he had only gotten it in the ass from only one of the men, and after all of his excitement this entire week of looking forward to this session, he definitely wanted it good, strong and long from both of his officers.

He had walked quite some distance into the deeper part of the park, and all of a sudden he saw one very quick red flash. He immediately knew that was his signal to stop, and he already knew from last week, —do not look back!

As he stopped in his tracks, he heard the familiar voice instruction yell, but only loud enough for him to hear, and not carry hardly any farther than just to Brad, "Stop, —drop em, and hit the deck, man!"

He did! He stopped, he pulled his shorts off, threw 'em on the ground and he immediately hit the deck! Face down, and not looking back! His ass, —filled with grease, was sticking up in the air, and was asking, no, —was actually begging, for action! Regardless of how much he attempted to calm it, his ass was, "out of control," and was actually wiggling in anticipation of some good hard cock action in it. Fortunately, "they" had once again picked a nice grassy area, although this grass really did need a good cutting. The entire park really needed some upkeep, but especially since this was quite a hidden area of the park, and was of course in a very seedy part of town, it really needed quite a lot of help. When Brad threw his shorts down, he managed to get them in just the right spot so that as he hit the deck, he would be able to lay his face directly on his shorts. He could not only smell his own body odors and the manly crotch scents emitting from his stretched and skin tight shorts, but he could also keep his face from laying directly on the tall grass. He did not want tall grass, itching and scratching his face, distracting from the actions that he was simply praying for, —back deep in his ass!

As he barely hit the deck, he heard two car doors close, and then to his complete and total shock, he heard two more doors close. "Four doors! Four people! Oh shit man! Four cops?!" Brad was now getting way, —way too excited!

"Oh shit man! Oh shit man!" He kept running through his head. "Four cops! Oh shit, am I going to get it from all four? Oh God! Is there four of them? Are four cops gonna fuck me!? Am I gonna get it from all four?"

"Yeah, that's Brad!" One of the, now, four cops said. I'd recognize that ass anywhere. Especially when it's bare! Hell, I think he has it bare more often, than not! I've seen it bare more than once, but until tonight, I've never seen it with any pants on it."

Brad's mind was now flipping. "Hell, whoever that is, he knows me, and I kind of think maybe he has fucked me, from what he is saying. Shit man, who is that?"

This was coming off way to similar to a gay porno flick, Brad thought. "One guy, all by himself, planning on meeting up with two hot and horny cops, but now turning out to be four, and meeting in a very sleazy and trashy part of town, in the deeper part of a rundown park, completely hidden from anybody, and actually too far away from anybody, for any person to hear him, if he needed to yell for some help for any reason."

The idea that he was meeting up with just a couple of horny, asshole loving cops, was starting to move way out beyond his normal thinking. This was starting to turn into something that was way more than he expected. Yeah, more than he expected, but nothing that he was wanting to run away from. He knew he was being used as the toy for some hot and horny cops, but he was real confused about the one that knew him. Was he a cop too? Or was he just some gay guy that the police were using to help find some hungry, horny, cop ready, gays, that the cops could use? He was really feeling like the central figure in a very hot, mysterious, and hunk filled drama story. He truly did want this night to turn out to be one hot fucking session, all centered around his hot and horny, and yeah, grease filled ass! He was getting way excited, and was willing to let himself be kind of totally out of any self-control, all to let himself, and his body, be used by four hot cops. He knew he was in a very dangerous part of town, in the "back lot" of a sleazy old city park, and was the object of four guys, but he was still not quite sure just yet if they were all cops or not. The one that knew him, still had him very confused.

His safety was all based on the fact that at least two of these guys were cops, and they did have a city cruiser with them. Excited, nervous and a lot of scared, since there were now more men involved than he had expected, Brad's only slight comfort was that he was sure no policeman would just let him lay there if everything got out of hand too badly. Brad knew he liked living the rougher and tougher life as far as the sexual actions were concerned, but to be completely removed from any safety factors and to be at the complete mercy of four men, without knowing what they intended, was making his heart beat harder and faster than it had for a very long time. He knew he wanted fucked, and he wanted to be fucked hard! He wanted to be treated like a strong man that can take abuse. He wanted to be the center of attention of four men that were bigger and stronger than he was, he wanted to know some of the city's finest were using him, using his body, and using his ass, and he knew that he was now experiencing all of the scary feelings of some guy that wants it "all", and has to live though the scare of not knowing if he is truly safe, just to get the thrills of delivering himself to their wants and desires.

Brad was starting to feel like a human, living, toy and although he knew he was at their complete mercy and that he was scared, he truly liked the way he felt. He liked the rush that was going through his body. He was getting very anxious for someone, any of those four, to start pounding on his ass. He wanted a cop up in his ass! He was getting so excited, he wanted the whole cop up in his ass! He wanted all of him! He wanted to get fucked, and he wanted it be a good rough cop fuck! He knew that he was now finally in a very unusual and questionable situation of submitting himself to men that he only hoped he could trust, in a very sleazy place, but he also knew this was a situation that he had dreamt of allowing himself to get into, for a long, long time now. He was now living a dream come true. This was reality! He was letting four hot, built, cops take him and use him, and, —all for their own personal pleasures. He was letting them have complete control over him, his body and his physical safety. He had never felt so completely removed from being his own self. He knew that he had just turned himself over to them as a hunk of meat, as if in the butcher's shop. He could only hope that he would not be treated the same as if they were in the butcher's shop and wanted to cut that hunk of meat all up into pieces.

In Brad's mind, "Cop one and cop two, I kind of know what they are like, but I really wonder what number three and number four are. And yeah, are they cops too? Oh man, let me find out real quickly! I hope they are cops and I hope they are all real hung, and really horny! I hope they really want to use me. If I live through this night, I want to know I gave all of them everything they were looking for. Right now I do want to be their bitch! I want them to use me!"

As Brad laid on the ground, with the four men towering above him, just wondering what was in store for him this night, he thought he heard a voice that sounded rather familiar to him.

"Yeah, guys, you guys found the right one! This is the one that I told you to keep an eye out for. I know damn well this one will do as we want.

Hell men, I've seen him do guys, and guys do him, that none of us would ever think about getting involved with! And doing stuff that none of us would ever come close to. I'm sure this pig will do it and go for it. He's got a real hungry asshole!"

That was the familiar voice. Immediately Brad started wondering just exactly what that person had in mind when he referred to him doing whatever they wanted him to do. All he knew was that right now he was still hoping that all four of them were planning on using him and his ass, and then he'd find out later what they were talking about. Right now he just wanted some cop-cock pushed up in his ass as far as possible. He really did not know why, but he did know that he liked getting fucked by a cop, more than by any other type of a guy. All he knew was that the idea of having a cop's cock rammed up in his ass, was more of a turn on than any other type of sexual action that he could ever imagine.

"OK Jack. Let's see how much he can take! Let's find out if he has got the staying power that we need or are we going to have to find us someone else."

That was another voice. One that Brad did not recognize and he was quite sure it was not from one of the officers that had fucked his ass, or his mouth, last week. He pondered the name Jack, and wondered if that was the name of the voice that he thought perhaps he did recognize, although if so, he still did not know who it belonged to.

"Brad," the familiar voice said. "This is Jack! The guy they refer to in the basement as "Big Jack." Your buddies in the basement don't know I'm a cop, and if you are smart, you won't tell them! If you like me, and everybody else that goes down there, using your ass, you'll keep it our own little secret. OK? I've fucked your ass before, and I'm going to fuck you again tonight, and my three buddies are gonna be using it too! George and Stan used you some last week and so they got me and Joe involved to see if you can take the working over that we need for our, "stand-by, man-ass." See guy, some of us cop guys have the need for some good tight, man-ass, and our last guy that we always used, kind of got himself all in trouble with the state police and got himself a nice little cell in the state prison, so he had to leave town. You can see, we need ourselves a new one. We don't fuck each other, well most of the time, anyway, so I told the guys who to watch out for, and last week George and Stan managed to find you and try you out. They told me they thought they had found the ass that I had told them about. They gave you a very good report. We decided to kind of audition you tonight and see if you are up to our standards and if so, let you know how you can help us out, whenever one of us have that need for a good tight "man-ass." See Brad, some of our cops have some pretty rough days, and they need a guy that they can get real rough on, to take some of their tension way before they go home and have to be nice and gentle on their women. So we need to see if you are the one that can really take a good long, hard and rough fucking from some pretty big and strong guys, or find out, if you are too much like the women that we need to be so soft with. Brad, all I can say right now is, if you like the idea of having some good, stiff, strong, cop-cock up in your strawberry colored ass, about every other night of the week, you had better play it smart tonight and not be some kind of a sissy weakling! We're looking for a guy that can take it regardless of how it is dished out. Understand?"

Big Jack! All of a sudden the voice that Brad thought he recognized, he realized belonged to the guy that had fucked his ass one night, about two months before, with what he knew was the biggest dick that he had ever had used on himself, and was the man that he had failed to turn and look at. Finally, Brad had "kind of" re-found the fucker that had that enormous big dick that he was so anxious to have rammed back up inside of his ass, again! Ever since that night, he had been so pissed at himself, that after he got that rough and hard fucking, that he did not find out who the guy was that had that dick, and how to get in-touch with him, so that he could get some more fucking from his enormous cock.

"Jack, I know who you are. Well, kind of! You're the guy that has got that great big thick dick, right? You fucked me one night in the bar basement! I was pushed up against the wall, and I was so whipped from taking it, that after you loaded my ass and gut with all your hot cum, I never turned around and looked at you, did I? I just laid there and leaned on the wall! I was totally beat! All I could do was lean on that wall and try to recover. You're the one that fucked the hell out of me that night aren't you? That was the night that some of my buddies had to help me get up the stairs, and in my buddy's car. I was fucking whipped that night! You fucked the hell out of me that night! I remember that and I remember that dick!"

"Yeah that's me. When I got you, I figured I had finally found me a good deep asshole that I could really use without having the other end yelling about how I was too big and how I hurt when I pushed it in. Your ass was hungry and I fed it everything I had! I fucked you rough that night! Tonight I'm going to test you again, and probably a little rougher this time, and my three buddies are going to be testing your ass too!"

"Oh God yeah!" Brad almost yelled back.

"So if you want to be our stand-by piece of ass, you had better make sure you open it up good and wide and beg for more, deeper and harder from each of us."

"Oh I will! Yeah I will! Yeah, please do me! Yeah please, please!" Brad pleaded!

"You ready to get started?" Jack asked of his hungry man laying on the ground. "We've got four big cop-cocks all stiffened up and ready. We're ready to do some testing. You willing to get it from all four of us!?"

"Oh God yes I am! I'm ready Jack, please somebody fuck me, please! Please fuck me! Yeah, yeah I want to be your fuck ass! I want to show you guys I can do it!"

"You think then that you are ready to see if you are man enough to be our ass of choice? All the other cops back at the precinct are anxious to see if we've found us some guy that is man enough to take care of all of them. They want a guy that likes it rough! They are cops, you know, and cops like to do it rough! Brad, if you can take us and what we are ready to give you tonight, you will never need to look for another fucker, for as long as you live in this town. You will have more cops wanting to fuck your sweet little ass than you can imagine. We are going to make you our precinct male whore! Our guys need to get their rocks off once in awhile, and it just might be up in your ass!"

"Oh God yes! Oh man please, yes!" Brad once again pleaded.

"I told the guys to keep an eye out for you, and last week everything started coming together, that is, if you are as much man back there as I remember from that night in the basement! Are you ready and willing? If you don't want to do this, now is the time to let us know. Once we get started man, it's your ass and we are going to be testing it out! You ready and willing? Now's the time, if you don't think you can take it. You remember how you got fucked in the basement that night? Well, this time there are four of us, and the other three like to fuck rough too. You willing?"

"Oh Jack please get somebody started on me man! Please Jack! Let somebody fuck me! I want to prove to you guys that I can take it. Please fuck me! Please somebody, please start fucking me!"

"Hey guys." Jack said to his three companions. "I kind of think maybe we have found our toy! I think maybe he is ready to become the ass of choice for all of us horny, hung, cops. What do you think?"

The other three cops, all with their hands on their stiff rods, stroking them back and forth, shook their heads in an affirmative action.

One of the three replied, "Well, I sure can say one thing. If we don't get started on him, and fill that hole of his, he is going to go crazy from frustration.

His ass is swinging in the breeze with just the idea that each of us are going to pump all of our cop juices in there and fill it up!"

"Oh God Jack! Oh shit man!" Brad pleaded! "Oh man I never dreamt that anything like this could ever happen to me! Please, —I want to be your precinct's ass slave! Oh Jack, I want to get fucked by all of the cops back there! I want them to use my ass! Oh God, yes Jack! Please, somebody start fucking me! Oh please! You guys, —pleeeaaase fuck me! Yes, —fuck me! Yes, —pleeeease fuck me, —pleeeeaaase!"

CHAPTER FOUR:

Yes I'm interested, Hell Yes I am!

Jack decided that he would be the first one on Brad's ass, and without any warning, he pounced down on Brad's butt and simply said, "Hang on buddy," as he grabbed his rod and pushed it up and into Brad's ass.

All Brad could think of for a few moments was, "Oh thank God I have an asshole full of grease!" Jack's aim was right on target and his full body weight went directly into his cock which then went directly into Brad's ass!

Brad heard one of Jack's companions actually exclaim, "Oh shit man! Oh my God! He went into him fast and hard! God he slammed his ass hard! Shit man, I'm not sure I could have done him that hard and that fast. Shit man, I hope that kid's ass is OK. Jack really rammed him with all of his might!"

Joe, the rather quiet one that had just been standing back and watching what was going on since they had arrived, replied to George, the man that had made the comments, that, "Jack told us that if this guy did turn out to be the one he thought it might be, that he wanted to be the first one in him to show us what this guy could take! He told me that the night he fucked him in that bar basement, this guy really took one hell of a lot more abuse in his butt than he had ever seen any other guy, ever take. He told me that after he found out how wild this guy can be, he tried his damnedest to get this kid to beg for him to stop, but he never did! He was still taking it, when Jack had to stop. Jack said he knew that if he ever got another chance with this kid, if he was all alone and with nobody else around, that he would have to be really careful that he did not get too carried away and hurt him some way. Jack told me that he does realize that he can get really turned on with some really wild sex, and playing with a guy, like this one is, and can be dangerous. He said that when one guy is the rough top, and especially when he is hung like he is, and the bottom guy takes more abuse than he should, things can get a little out of hand. He said this guy just does not protect himself at all, and if a guy can do it to him, he will take more than he should. Jack said that he knows he does have an oversized dick, and this kid was really all turned on and excited about him getting really rough, with it up in his ass. He told me that, during that night in the basement, he only stopped because he heard some of the other guys down there, that night, making comments about how they might have to step in and stop what was happening. That's what made him realize that he was probably getting way to rough on the kid. He said he wanted to be first, so that he could show us how aggressive we could get with him. And believe me, with the size of a dick that Jack has got, right now, that kid has to know he has got one fucking train, running back an forth,—in and out of his ass! I got fucked by Jack once, and that was the last time. I fucking screamed my lungs out when he rammed that think up in me. I got him out and told him never again. We've remained friends, but let me tell you I have never let him fuck my ass again. Has he ever fucked you?"

"Oh yeah! Oh yeah, he has!" George replied. "Yeah he did one night after we had been out drinking together. Let me tell you, when he pushed that damn big thing up in me, it sure did take care of my being kind of drunk. It sobered me up real quickly! Hell, I kept checking my asshole for three days after that to see if it was bleeding yet. It never did, but it sure as hell sure felt like it should have."

Stan, the officer that had fucked Brad's ass the week before, looked at George and Joe and rather surprisingly said, "You are kidding me! You two do not like getting fucked by Jack? Shit man, I thought you guys got it as often as possible from him. Shit man! I like it, and I keep telling him to fuck me deeper. I thought you guys got fucked by him all of the time. Shit, I get him to fuck me at least once or twice a week. Shit man, I like it. Well, anyway, you two sure did have me fooled. I thought you two were using him as much as I do. Well, —I guess that will just mean that I will have to give him my ass to use that much more often."

Jack could hear the conversation going on above his head, and he slightly turned toward Stan, grinned a broad grin, and just said, "Yeah!"

"Well, I guess that plan does not upset Jack any, does it?" Joe said with a grin, as he looked toward Stan. "Sounds like that, oversized, big dick, fuck happy, cop guy, will be using you and this kid just as often as he can. I had no idea you two were doing it together. I guess when I told him to never put it back in my ass, I guess I just never stopped to figure out who he was fucking. I guess I must had just thought his wife was getting it more often now."

All three men that had been discussing their sessions of getting fucked by Jack, had all been standing there stroking their respective hard-ons as they talked and watched Jack fuck the hell out of Brad's tight white ass.

"Hey this kid sucked me off last week, and I'm going for it again, now!" George suddenly announced as he planted himself directly in front of Brad's face and told him to open up for some "nice fine dinning!"

Brad immediately opened his mouth in an attempt to get George's dick in it, but with the rough and tumble action that was still going on in his ass, he had trouble lining his mouth and George's dick up together. George grabbed his eight and one half inch, cop's meat stick and fed it into Brad's mouth. Brad immediately closed his mouth down on it and trapped it inside with force and pressure, so that the movement going on in his asshole did not force it to pop out of his mouth.

Stan and Joe watched as one of their co-workers fucked the hell out of a horny, young 20's something "kid", as they called him, and another co-worker fed that same kid his entire length of cock meat. Stan and Joe were both stroking their respective hangs of meat when without warning Stan knelt down and grabbed Joe's bag of balls, forcing his dick to drop down far enough for Stan to quickly put it in his mouth!

"Shit man!" Joe exclaimed. "I thought we were all out here to fuck around with this kid. I didn't know we were going to be doing each other."

Stan kind of just uttered something like, "Yeah, Yeah", and then pulled Joe's body up close to his face so that he could get onto Joe's meat as far as possible. Joe accepted the fact that although he did not expect anything like this to happen between any of the cops, he accepted it, and obviously started to really enjoy it since he grabbed ahold of Stan's head and pulled him forward, and onto the full depth of his dick. Suddenly he started yelling, "Yeah man! Yeah! Suck me! Suck me! Oh God Stan, make me cum!"

Everybody except Brad grinned and looked at Joe. All of them were very surprised to hear that coming out of Joe's mouth since he was always the quiet one. They did not expect to hear him express any type of excitement, especially to hear him beg for Stan to make him cum.

Joe saw everybody looking at him and grinning. He looked at them and said, "Hey man! I don't get sex out in the city parks like you guys do all of the time. This is new and exciting to me, OK? Nobody can hear us way back here anyway! Suck me Stan!"

The other officers had just experienced what, they thought, might be a complete break through in a personality change. Joe just had never been the type of a guy that any of them could expect that type of action from. They were happy to see the change.

Jack was torturing Brad's ass. The action that night in the bar basement was turning out to be rather calm, compared to what the city officer was doing to him, this night! Late at night, out under the moon light, showing off in front of his sex buddies, playing with some young smaller sized kid, in the back of an old and trashy city park, simply gave Jack that much more excitement of being an, —out of control wild and native animal! It just built that much more excitement inside of himself to make him try, and force Brad to beg for some relief. He had a challenge on his hands. Brad was not giving in. He was getting the treatment that he had dreamt of having or at least wanted to get for years now, and he certainly was not going to stop it. Brad did not know why, but he did know that he had an internal desire to be sexually beaten up by somebody bigger and stronger than he was, and for that person to be a cop, was a complete sexual excitement and turn-on for him. He was living a dream that he thought could only be made up. He knew his body was being pretty well beaten up, but he also knew that this could only happen to a guy once in his life, if at all, and tonight was his night to stick it out, and be stronger than he could have ever imagined himself to be. He knew he was proving to himself that although he was just slightly, as of about a month ago, 22 years old, and his 145 pound frame and body certainly did not match up to the size of any of these cops, he was not going to allow himself to even hint that he needed to stop. He knew he had Jack in his ass, and that Jack was without doubt the roughest of the group, and that he wanted Jack to collapse on him, in a complete pile of exhaustion, before he even thought of begging for some relief. He mentally accepted the outrageous rampage that was going on in his ass by fully concentrating on the dick in his mouth. He grabbed George and pulled him forward and into his mouth as fully as he could. His entire attention was geared toward that dick. He knew his ass was being used harder and rougher than it had ever been before, but knowing that he was letting it all happen, simply for the personal pleasure of the hot cop fucking him, was a total payoff for the possible injures that he knew he might be receiving back there. He knew his insides were OK. His butt might end up being kind of black and blue, but to be able to give himself so totally and so completely, to such a hunky group of guys, —and cops too, —was more than a privilege. He did not know of any other guy, that he had ever heard of, that had been fucked by four cops in one night! He had never even seen a gay porno that was more exciting than this! He felt like his ass was really the star of some, yet to be produced, video! As he thought that, all of a sudden he truly was wishing that there was a film crew somewhere, somewhere, hidden in the bushes, filming him and all of the cops that were fucking him, roughing him up, and playing with him!

Brad had kind of, 'figured out,' the group that was so completely using him, and all parts of him, out in this old trashy city park. He did already know Jack. That one he had finally figured out. He had the advantage of remembering him from the bar basement and he definitely remembered his very wrestler type of a body. Guessing, —he guessed that Jack might be in his late 20's. A very thick chest, probably a 52 or a 53" chest. Tiny waist line of about maybe a 34", and probably weighed in at 220 or 230, but he knew he was not too sure about that. Brad had never had much experience with a real muscular hunky and bulky type of a guy before, so guessing some guy's weight that was built like that was more of a guess for him.

Since George had made the comment about getting sucked off by this guy a week ago, he knew he was one of the two original cops. Last week when George was in front of him, Brad was not given any time or chance to look up at his face. Now that Brad had a slight chance to check him out, he decided that George was, in Brad's assumptions, about 34 years old, stood about 6' 1 or 2, and probably weighed in at about 190 pounds of very cop like solid muscles. He did not see him naked last week, since he had then only dropped his uniform pants enough to get sucked on, but tonight he got a chance to see the entire nice and well formed, athletic body. He was especially appreciating the view of being so very close to George's mid section. He saw a great six-pack!

He knew Stan had been his fucker, the week before. He recognized his voice, and he was anxious to have Stan take his turn, in his ass, this night. His fucking last week by Stan had been enjoyable, and he was looking forward to it again. After having a chance to see Stan this week, —last week he was never allowed to look at him, he decided that Stan might be about 42 or 43 years old, probably about 5'11" tall, and probably weighed in at close to 200 pounds. He had a much more mature body than George did, but none the less, he was still a very hot built guy. Just not as tight of a skin coating, as when comparing it to George.

Joe was the new one to him. He had never seen Joe before tonight. Joe looked to be a lot more like maybe 34 or 35. Tall and very lanky body. Probably 6' 4 tall, and probably weighed in at 180 or 190 pounds. The very first thing that Brad did notice about Joe was the size of his feet. Yes, the old saying stood true as far as Brad was concerned. Joe's hard-on was the longest of the group. Not the thickest, but definitely the longest. Probably a good nine or nine and a half inches long. Enough to make Brad get real anxious to have him pushing it up in his ass, and all of the way!

Jack was sweating, even though it was not a very hot or humid night out. As the sweat dripped onto Brad's back, he knew that Jack was starting to get kind of winded from the frantic attach that he was giving Brad's ass. Brad laid there and continued to enjoy George's meat that he was so happily sucking on as strongly as he could.

Suddenly George pulled his cock out of Brad's mouth and said, "Whoa man! You were getting me way too close to cumin, and I don't want to do that until I've had my turn in that cute little ass of yours. You were really sucking me like you have done that to guys for years. You really know how to suck, don't ya?!"

Jack suddenly laid down on Brad's back and asked George if he was ready to "Take over back here? I've fucked this ass as hard as I can fuck an ass, and I guess this one must be made out of steel! I thought for sure that since I would be laying down on top of him tonight, instead of standing up, like I did that night in the bar basement, that I could fuck him hard enough to make him beg for mercy, but shit man, I was wrong! I don't think there is anything that can make this kid yell for help. I have never, in my entire life, ever fucked some guy as hard and as rough as I have this one and not had the guy cry for me to stop. I give up! All I can say is he sure is my choice for being our new precinct whore. Hey George, fuck his ass!"

Jack got up, George laid down, and George took over the "responsibility" of being the group's fucker for a while. He did not fuck Brad as roughly as Jack had just done, but he was definitely in the mood. He grabbed ahold of Brad's chest and pulled himself up and into Brad as fully as he could. He hung on tight to Brad's chest and humped his butt in a good steady rhythm.

"Fuck me, fuck me!" Brad begged. It was obvious to all of the cops that their little sex toy, was having the time of his life.

"Shit man! I have never seen some guy take it like this one does!" Stan said. "And I have been around a lot of guys getting fucked! I haven't been in his butt yet, but from what I have already seen, I know for damn sure he is the one we need as our precinct whore. We need to take care of this one and make sure he gets everything he needs."

Stan and Joe had broken up their tight little sucking session, and when George moved away from in front of Brad, Joe took his place. Knowing that Joe was swinging the longest cock of the group, Brad broke out in a big smile as he squatted in front to Brad and rather "offered" his stick of meat to Brad's mouth. Brad immediately said, "Yeah", and put it in his mouth. The extra length of this dick forced Brad to readjust himself so that he could comfortably take all of it without choking. He did not want to choke or gag in front of any of these guys. He was still on his main mission of proving to all of them that he could do whatever they did, or offered, for him to do. He truly wanted to leave this session, feeling like he was the winner. He knew he was younger, smaller and probably much less experienced than any of these cops, but he wanted to be the one that everybody admired for his abilities with another man. He wanted to actually feel like he had completely grown up this night! He wanted to show all of 'em, that he might be smaller, but he can be just as rough and tough as any of 'em, and especially during sex! He wanted to show them, he could take it!

Stan watched George get into Brad's ass, and he watched as Joe stuck his rod into Brad's mouth, and he then turned to Jack and said, "Well man! Your dick has not shot off yet, and my ass is apparently the only other ass besides the kid that will allow you in it, so how about you fuck me? I did not know until tonight that those two wimps do not get fucked by you, so I guess the kid and I will be your main holes to keep filled. Come on Jack, pump my ass like you did the kid's!"

Stan bent over, grabbed his ankles, and Jack came up behind him as if he was the stallion mounting his mare. One push, and Stan was full. Full and happy. He liked getting it in the ass from Jack, and now that he understood that not all of the group used that dick, that made him that much more happy, that he will be able to openly ask for it more often than he has in the past.

Brad got fucked by George in a nice and calmly manner, and accepted his ass full of cum when George could not hold it anymore! George pulled his dick out, wiped it across Brad's back and then asked who wanted to do "this ass" next.

Joe moved from his "getting sucked" position to his, "I will fuck him" position, and Brad now got Joe's dick in the opposite end. Again, one steady push and Joe was completely and deeply all inside. Brad turned his head and said, "Thanks!" Brad wanted each of his tops to know that he appreciated having each one of them up inside of himself. He wanted them to know that he was trying his best to be their toy of pleasure and joy. He wanted each of them to be real anxious to re-do this entire session real soon. He did not know if it would ever happen for the whole group to be together and play with him as a group again, but to be looked at as the guy any of them can call at any time to get some good ass, was his aim. He did not want any of the four to regret being there that night.

Joe made more of a love session out of his fucking than the other men had done. He caressed Brad's body more intently, and he ran his tongue up and down Brad's neck and shoulders. He blew into Brad's ears. He talked to Brad as he fucked his ass. He told him how glad he was that he had a chance to fuck such a good tight and young ass. He told Brad that he was hoping that they would be having a lot more fuck sessions together, and he was the only man that asked Brad if he ever played the top roll. Brad was surprised when he asked him that, since everybody had only been acting interested in using him as a bottom fixture. Nobody else had seemed to care if he was only a meat item to be rammed, or if he liked to be the top man once in awhile.

"Yeah Joe, yeah. I like being on top too. Everybody at the bar has always known me as almost strictly a bottom guy, since I've been getting fucked in that basement since I was a few years younger. That bar was owned by another guy back then, and he was really into bottoms, so that is how I got in there, and how I got introduced to the basement. He was the one that first suggested that I spend some time down there, kinda maybe just hang out, all undressed, and he'd have some guys bring something down for me to drink. He knew which guys were major tops, and he knew that once they found me down there all bare, it was gonna be a go from that point on! So anyway, over the years, I've gotten known as "the" bottom hole to use. But, whenever I get a chance, I like to do the fucking too."

"Hey great!" Joe replied. "I like to get my ass fucked too, and I think you just might be the guy to do it for me. What do you think? I don't mean tonight, but sometime soon over at my place, OK?"

"Yeah, hell yeah!" Brad quickly replied. "You don't let Jack fuck you?"

"No, no! No I don't! I will tell you I have no idea in the whole world how in the hell you can take it so roughly from him. He is too damn rough for me, especially with that big rod he uses. No, he tried once, and I wanted him to try, but I had to tell him never again. Too much and too rough! Now you, I think that could be fun!"

Jack could hear what the conversation had been between Joe and Brad, and with a big grin on his face he asked, "Hey you two. Are you going to just lay there and talk the rest of the night, or are you going to get some fucking done?"

Joe turned, looked toward Jack and answered. "Hey big man. The way you fucked the skin off of this guy tonight, I decided that he needed some rest and some nice relaxation for a change. I've got my dick up in him. He can feel it. Just because it's an asshole and I've got a dick stuck up in it, we don't have to act like some hurricane is happening. You fuck Stan over there, and I will fuck our boy over here. OK?"

"Well Joe, my man!" Jack replied. "The way you are fucking, it will take you a year and a half to build yourself up to a cum. Your dick can't even tell it's in a guy's ass!"

Joe looked toward Jack and just rather laughed at his comment.

Joe continued to fuck Brad's ass until all at once he asked Brad if he could shoot a load up in him. "I'm getting real close. I'm about ready to give you a kid. Brad, can I shoot off in you? I'm ready to cum!"

"Yeah, let me feel it! Yeah, let me feel your juices man! Let me take home some good hot police juices! Yeah, unload in me!"

Joe dropped his load, and then relaxed his body across Brad's. When Stan saw that Joe was done fucking, he told Joe to move, so that he could get his turn in Brad's ass, and he told Jack to get up on his back, so that Jack could fuck him, while he fucked Brad. He and Jack could be fucking, all at the same time. Jack mounted Stan and ran his pole up into his ass.

Brad had now been fucked by three of the four guys, and as soon as Stan got up in him, he knew he would have taken all four of the cops, and with Stan getting fucked by Jack, —as he fucked Brad, —he kind of felt like he was actually getting fucked by two guys all at the same time. He liked the idea that Stan was in him, and Jack was in Stan. Brad simply knew that any activity, that was off of the straight and narrow, was definitely to his liking! He was always into any kink! He always wanted something different and just a little more off beat! This night of getting fucked out in a city park by four city policemen was tops for him. Outdoors! In a public park! No walls, and anybody could come walking up and see him getting it in the ass! And getting it in the ass by cops! This was the kind of living that he always wanted. Did not happen often enough, but he figured that if he was gutsy enough, he could maybe find it once in awhile. This time it really worked. And, he had been hearing these cops talk about making him the precinct whore, if he met the test, and since he really did feel like maybe he even went past the test, he was wondering just what all of that talking meant. "The precinct's whore!? Used by all of 'em? On call for all of the hot cops in the precinct? They'd all have his number, and be able to call him whenever they needed to get a nut off!?" Oh, man he loved the thought!

Suddenly he realized that he had a man in his ass, and he had gotten all carried away thinking about the precinct whore thing, and had forgotten that he was still getting fucked! And by a guy that was also getting fucked. That he liked!

Brad was not too sure if Stan was doing much actions and motions in his ass, but he sure did know that both he and Stan were feeling the effects of Jack being on the ultimate top. Jack was fucking Stan, just as wildly as he had fucked Brad!

Brad was truly enjoying the double stack fucking that he was the bottom for, when all of a sudden, and without warning, Jack started yelling that he was going to be cumin!

"Me too!" Stan yelled. "I'm gonna cum! Jack get off of me! Jack I'm going to cum! Jack let me off, so I can cum!"

Stan was wanting to pull out of Brad before he came, but Jack was so forceful in pushing on Stan's butt, —as he came, that Stan had no choice but to shoot his load into Brad's ass! Brad understood what was happening, and he told Stan that he really wanted to keep Stan in him when he shot off. "Stan, I wanted to feel your load hit my insides. I wanted you in there! Thanks man, I wanted to feel you unload in me! Thanks! That is what I wanted!"

After Jack and Stan both shot their loads, everybody rather separated and attempted to re-coup some.

As everybody laid there, collecting their thoughts, Brad asked. "Hey men. Is it OK if I beat off. I've not had a chance tonight to unload my load. Can I do that?"

All four cops suddenly gasped and Jack said, "Oh shit man! We never thought about him needing to shoot off. Hell yes Brad, jerk it man! Oh God man! We were so totally consumed in our own affairs and desires, we never thought about making sure he got what he needed. Brad jerk it man. You need some help?"

"Hey, if you are offering, —of course I'm not going to say no! I love having your hands on me, all of you guys! I love it!"

Jack moved over toward Brad and took Brad's dick in his hand and started jerking on it. It got harder than it already was, and Jack could tell that it was not going to take very much action to make the head of it shoot out its load. Stan came over and started squeezing and biting Brad's left tit, and then motioned for George to come over and play with the other one. Joe did not want to be left out of the action, so he joined the group and grabbed ahold of Brad's bag of balls, and reached back and under, and stuck a finger up and in Brad's ass.

"Oh shit man! Oh God! Oh God this is great!" Brad kept screaming. "Oh God, oh shit! Oh God! Yeah, pinch my tits! Yeah, pinch them tight! Slap my balls! Yeah men, get rough with me! Do me! Play with me! Bite me! Guys, bite my tits! Please! Oh yeah, Oh yeah this is great! Oh men, I'm about ready to cum. Men, I'm about ready to let it fly! Oh here it comes! Oh, —I'm cumming, —I'm cumming, —I'm cumming!"

And he did! Everybody that was playing with him at that time, all of the cops, were amazed at how far he shot his wad! The shot flew more than five feet out in front of them.

"Oh shit!" Two of them exclaimed. "Shit man, —did you see how damn far that shot flew?"

"Shit, I wish I had gotten that up in my ass!" Joe said. "Shit man that would have felt fucking good! God, I wish I had been getting fucked by him when that let loose! God I would have loved to feel that landing up inside of me!"

Everybody was totally amazed at Brad's shot and how he kept begging everybody to keep getting rougher and rougher with him. The way he wanted to be pinched, bit and really man-handled, really turned all of them on!

"OK guys!" Jack rather announced. "I kind of think Brad has done a little more than hit our goals. I think he is going to be the precinct's new male-whore. Any objections?"

All of the other policemen just shook their heads, "No."

"OK then, Brad are you willing to be our new precinct male whore and make yourself available to all of us whenever we need to use you? We have a secret apartment available to us, and you will be free to use that space any time you want, as long as you are willing to bend over and get it up the ass from any policeman that wants it. We've got something like 15 or 20 different officers that are in on this secret apartment arrangement, and all of them carry keys for it. Tall guys, short guys, big guys, white guys, black guys, —just about every description I can say, and one of 'em is a Captain! He's good, you'll like taking care of him, and you know what they say about black men! Especially black cops! We've got two of them that usually patrol together, and then, they go get their fun together! So hang on man, —I know that pretty damn soon, you're gonna have two of the hottest looking black cops this side of the Rock Mountains, in bed with you, and at the same time! They do it together, cause they like it rough! They use the whore-boy, if I can call you that, and then they use each other to get everything out and going, that they need to get done before they go home to their wives! For them, you better save some time, and I don't mean just an hour!"

"We'll pay you some, —under the table, spending money so that you can keep your current apartment, and we'll expect you to carry a cell phone so that our guys can get ahold of you at all times. We'll give you the phone. The only time that you can be excused from being available, at request, is while you are at work. OK? Some of the calls may come in during the middle of the night, since we get off of work at all hours. Some of them might have some rather weird ideas of what they expect the precinct whore to do with them, but after knowing you tonight, I really don't think any of them will be asking for anything more than you are willing to give. In-fact, maybe some of them will introduce you to some new stuff that you have never done before, and knowing some of the stuff you've been involved in, you just might show some of the guys some stuff that they've never done before! They find out about you, some of 'em just might come to you, to learn some stuff that they've heard about, but never done. Well, —yet, that is! There will be times when there will be more than just one guy at a time wanting attention, and we will depend on you to try every attempt possible to make all of them happy, and not leave anybody out. Your pay-back for being our whore is your total sexual freedom anywhere at any time in this town. Even if we find you getting a complete fucking in the middle of downtown, out on the street, we might act like we are arresting you, but it will all be, a complete show. If you agree, from this night on, as long as you are our precinct's male-ass, you don't have to worry about you and your playmate getting busted for having sex out in public. We have a common agreement with the other precincts that have their own precinct's whores. How does this sound to you? Interested?"

"Hell yes I am interested! Shit yes I'm interested! Yes, I'm interested. Hell yes, I am! This means I will have an automatic list of about 15 or 20 cops that I can depend on to come by and fuck my ass? Hell yes, I am interested! How do I get started?"

"Well, if you agree to this, then the first thing we need to do is take you to the apartment and let you know where the hideout is located. Now you have to remember, that apartment is a secret. Total secret! Do not tell anybody about it! Not even your fuck buddies! OK?"

"Yeah, of course! No, I won't let anybody else know about it. I promise! Oh my God, my own private space to use to just get fucked by cops! Oh shit man, I can't believe this! I'm gonna be the only guy that you guys will be using, and for any of the other policemen to use, whenever they need to use me? Right? Is that right!?"

"Right, —you are right! You do it right, and I'm sure you will be getting it up in the ass at least once a day by one of the city's finest! And once you have had them all in bed and fucking that sweet little ass of yours, I'm sure you will agree they are the finest! And, in more ways than one! OK, Joe is gonna take you over there now. He's the only single guy in the group, so he'll be your contact person. Do not call any of the officers' houses, —understand? Everybody else is a married man, and they all have families. You need to protect them, or you are out! Out! Understand?"

"Oh shit yes, I do! Yes, I completely do understand!"

"OK guys!" Jack said. "I guess our night is over. We've all tested Brad, and checked his ass and his actions out, and I think all of us will agree that he is going to make a nice, little ass, addition to our group. Joe, take Brad with you and help him start getting organized. He needs to be ready when one of our city's finest gives him a call or stops by that apartment. And besides, they are anxious to see if we found ourselves a good tight ass that is willing to be used and re-used!"

Looking at Brad, Jack added, "Brad, we haven't had a precinct whore for a few weeks now, and I know damn well that some of our men are a little more than anxious to get back into some guy's ass, so I'm telling you right now, be ready, cause I'm sure that for probably the next four or five days, you are not gonna have any time to even get out of bed! Your ass is gonna be fucking busy, and I do mean busy! Those guys in blue are fucking hungry, and it's not for beans!"

"OK, come on Brad!" Joe instructed. "You are about to enter a completely new and exciting life, —taking care of more horny cops, and their cock needs, —more, horny for a guy's tight little ass, than the city probably even realizes that they have. Let's get you all set up! I think maybe I will just happen to be your first "client," after we get to the apartment tonight. I need to get fucked and do some more fucking! You are our whore now, —remember?!"

"Don't worry Joe! I'd jump right back in bed with you, or any of you guys, right now, —even if I wasn't the precinct whore! Let's go, I'm ready! I'm really fucking ready! You know, even being a real active gay guy that likes to really get it in the ass as often as possible, I never wanted to be called a whore, but now, knowing that it's for 15 or 20, hot, hung and built like hell, city cops, it fits man, it fits!"

ONE HOT COP, OFFICER GREG

CHAPTER ONE:

It Died and it Won't Start!

"Hey man, what's going on here?" Greg Hudson, —'Officer Greg Hudson'— asked, as he pulled up beside a disabled older Chevy sedan and its very, very frustrated driver.

"Oh this damn thing!" Shawn replied as he looked over at the Highway officer and said, "Shit man! I've had this thing into the shop about three times trying to find out what in the hell is wrong with it, and they can't find a damn thing wrong with it, and now it's doing it again!"

"Well, what happened?" Officer Hudson asked. "Did it just die on you here at the stop sign?"

"Yeah, it did. I stopped here and all of a sudden it died and it won't start. The garage told me that they really can't do anything to it until they can get to it when it's acting up, and of course, I'm never at the garage when it happens."

"How long you been here?" The officer inquired.

"Oh shit, —probably about half an hour! I've tried everything with it trying to get it to run again, and it just will not! I don't know what in the hell I am gonna do now! Crap man, — miles and miles from home and this does it again! What in the hell am I going to do?" Shawn said in much more frustration than as a question.

As Officer Greg Hudson leaned up against the side of Shawn's car, he stuck out his hand and introduced himself and continued. "Well, I sure can't do too much to the car for you, but if you can decide what you need to do, I'll be more than glad to help you out, however I can. What do you want to do?"

Shawn introduced himself to Officer Hudson, and after some real frustrations, finally decided that if there was some repair shop someplace close by that Office Hudson could recommend, then he thought maybe he needed to have 'em come out and tow it in, and see what they could do to it.

"Shit man, I knew I should have dumped this old thing before heading out for Denver, but since it hasn't done this for awhile, I thought it'd be OK. Damn it, why in the hell didn't I get rid of this pile of shit?!"

"Well Shawn," Office Hudson consoled. "Look at it this way. At least you don't have a car full of kids with you giving you additional problems. Things could be worse, man. If I broke down, I'd have three kids and my wife, all hot, hungry and all needing to go to the bathroom all at once."

Looking over at the officer and putting a big grin on his face, Shawn replied, "Hell yeah man! I'm not married and don't have any kids, so I didn't look at it that way. It would be a big fucking problem if I had a car full of kids! That is for damn sure!"

"Oh I'm sorry!" Office Hudson replied. "I guess I rather assumed that was a wedding ring you had on. So, anyway, I sure didn't mean to get you all married off without you knowing it!"

Shawn kind of looked down at his hand and then rather attempted to explain, "Well, yeah you are kind of right. That's a partnership ring. Guess maybe I am married, just not to a woman. Understand?"

"Oh, I'm sorry! I didn't mean to intrude in your personal life! Yeah, I understand!"

"Thanks!" Shawn replied with somewhat of a depressed sound in his voice. "So what do you suggest? Any dependable repair shops around that I could call? Damn this pisses me off!"

"Yeah, Shawn. Springerhill is right down this road about 7 or 8 miles and I know those guys, and you can trust them. Want me to get them on my cell phone and see if they can come out here and try to see what they can do?"

"Yeah Officer, I guess so! I really don't know what else I can do. I'm just pissed at myself right now. Damn it man, I kept telling Rog that I needed to dump this thing, but then it quit doing this, so I trusted it too much! Yeah, do you mind calling them and seeing if they can help me?"

Greg got his personal cell phone out of his cruiser, slowly walked around to the front of his cruiser and made a call to J&G's Garage. He had a short conversation, which Shawn could not hear, he then hung up, and came back to the side of the car and turned to Shawn.

"Hey Shawn, here's the deal. Jay is headed out this way. He's bringing the tow truck just in case he needs it, but he is going to try and get you running without towing you in. He'll be here in about 15 or 20 minutes, and I need to get going, so I told him to let me know what happens. He knows my phone number and he's going to give me a call and fill me in on if he has to tow you in or not! OK?"

"Yeah, thanks a lot! I really do appreciate it Sir! Thanks a lot!"

"Oh Shawn you're welcome, but don't call me Sir! I appreciate it, and I like it, but when a guy like you does that, I kind of start loosing it, so just call me Greg, —OK?"

As Office Hudson got into his cruiser and started the engine, Shawn said, "Yeah, OK. Thanks though, —thanks for the help Sir, I mean Greg! Thanks a lot!"

"Hey Shawn, I'm sure I'll be talking to you again. Jay'll take good care of you. He should be here real soon, OK?"

"Yeah thanks again!" Shawn yelled as he waved "Bye" to the officer as he pulled away!

Shawn stepped back against the side of his car, leaned on the front fender and pondered the statement of why Office Hudson did not want Shawn to call him "Sir". 'Don't call me Sir! I appreciate it, and I like it, but when a guy like you does that, I kind of start loosing it, so just call me Greg, OK?' That statement really made Shawn very confused. "Shit man!" Shawn told himself. "Crap I wish his statement of, —when a guy like you, does that, I kind of start loosing it,—meant that he liked to be called 'Sir' or even maybe 'Daddy' by a guy like me. Oh shit man! Hell, he knows I'm gay! I told him about Rog! Suppose he was kind of hitting up on me? Suppose he was trying to tell me something? Oh shit man, —forget it! He is too fucking hot of a looking cop to be playing around with someone like me. Besides he mentioned his wife and kids. Shawn, drop your wishing! The guy was just being nice. Looking damn good in those ass tight, patrol officer pants that hugs every moving muscle in his body, —but he's just being nice. Every time I see some of those tight fitting, tight hugging, officer pants, hugging some big long dick, sticking out just a little, or, on some cops, a lot, I just get all turned on! Damn how I'd love to just slam my face up in that crotch and feel his dick pushing back on my face! Just lick my tongue up and down that bulge! But hey man,

—every hot looking guy is not trying to get in your pants, or get you into his pants. Especially an officer of the law! Yeah, even those guys that have got the crotches showing like they do! Hot looking guys, right, but that sure don't mean they all want to play around with some other guy! Sure as hell wish it did, but it don't, —so just forget it!"

Just as Shawn was attempting to quit wishing and hoping that Greg was trying to hit up on him, he saw a tow truck approaching and then pulling in, off of the side of the roadway, behind his car.

Jay got out of the truck, introduced himself to Shawn, as Shawn did in return. For about ten or fifteen minutes Jay had his head stuck under the hood of Shawn's car, all in feeble attempts of getting it to start.

Finally with both hands resting on the raised hood of the car, and his head hung down, Jay finally told Shawn that he was not going to be able to get it started out there in the country, he needed to get it into the garage when he could get it up on the hoist and where he had better tools.

After getting the car hooked up to the tow truck, Jay and Shawn climbed into the cab of the truck and headed for the garage.

The two men exchanged some small talk on the drive into town, but Shawn certainly did find the part about Officer Hudson being the most interesting. Jay did seem to be very interested in finding out exactly what Greg and Shawn had talked about while they were together. Jay asked some rather unusual questions as far as Shawn was concerned. Jay had asked if he and Greg had ever met before, or did Greg just happen to be coming down that road and find Shawn stranded there. Jay had asked if Greg had perhaps made any mention about another guy that not too long ago also had some car troubles and was rather forced to stay in town over night until they could get a car part. Jay also asked if he was traveling by himself or was there anybody else someplace that needed to be called or picked up someplace. Shawn did notice that more than just once Jay had made some pretty strong comments about how nice of a guy Greg was and how he always appreciated having him around, whenever possible. About the only comment that Shawn exchanged about Officer Hudson was what he thought was the rather strange comment and request about not calling him "Sir". He did tell Jay that Office Hudson had made a comment that being called "Sir" made him rather start loosing it, and he certainly did not quite understand that.

Jay simply looked over at Shawn, ginned, and continued the confusion in Shawn's mind with a comment of, "Well Shawn, I certainly can understand Greg and that comment. Don't worry about it!"

The two men arrived at the garage and after getting the car un-hooked from the tow truck, Jay introduced Shawn to his company partner George.

After hand pushing Shawn's car into the service bay, George left the auto that he had been working on, and he and Jay attacked Shawn's car as a team. Shawn found some magazines to browse through and a coke machine where he retrieved a good cold drink from.

About 45 minutes later, Jay finally came into the waiting room, and said, "OK, formal announcement! You are here till tomorrow! Your fuel pump is shot! It is dead! I can understand why the other guys couldn't figure it out for you, but it finally took its last breath. We thought a couple of times that we had it fixed too, then it went bonkers again. It finally did the death kick. We've got to get you a rebuilt pump from Denver and the quickest it can be here is by about 10 am tomorrow. What kind of problems is that going to be for you?"

"Oh shit! Crap! Hell, I was supposed to be in Denver tonight myself! Crap! Well, I guess I need to find someplace to sleep for the night and then leave whenever you guys can have it ready! Crap! Got any hotels or motels in this town?"

"Yeah we do, but let me call Greg first to see if he can do anything for you before you take off for the hotel, OK?"

"Well yeah, I guess!" Shawn answered with a major question in his voice. He had no idea at all why Greg should be involved, other than he had told Jay to call him and tell him how everything was going.

Jay dialed the phone, without looking up a number, and talked to Greg. He told Greg about the fuel pump and how Shawn was going to need to stay in town over night. After a lot of Yeahs, a lot of OK's and a lot of Uh-huhs, Jay said one final OK and then hung up the phone.

"Greg's on his way over here. Said he's got a place for you to stay at tonight."

With total confusion, Shawn tried to find out just why Officer Hudson would be so interested in what was happening, but he really did not get any good answers from Jay nor George. Finally he decided to just kind of kick back and wait for Officer Hudson to show up and then find out just what was happening. Shawn pondered the very confusing statement, "He's got a place for you to stay tonight! What in the hell does he mean by that? What, is he going to take me home to his house and let me sleep there? He's got a family to worry about and hell he don't know me! This is too damn confusing!"

Only about 25 minutes later, Office Hudson drove into the garage drive, got out of his car, approached Shawn and said, "Hey Shawn, —Jay said you'll have to stay in town till they get the fuel pump tomorrow, right?"

Shawn looked at the officer and just replied, "Yeah."

"Hey Shawn, let's you and me take a little walk over here and have a little talk, OK?"

Shawn looked at the officer and remaining in a complete state of confusion, he agreed to the walk and talk. Why, he certainly did not know, but none the less Officer Hudson wanted to, so he had no great reason to refuse.

The two men, one a hunky hot looking Highway Patrol officer, and one poor traveler with a broken down car, started a slow walk over toward a field area that was away from other buildings and other people.

The site of the two men walking together would have been a great photo shoot for any men's ad, for any man's product. One man, the Highway Patrol Officer was a man of about age 35 or 36, standing six foot one or two, sporting a chest of about 50" and a waist of only about 34, weighing a very stout and strong armed weight room body of about 210 pounds, and of course supporting the very familiar standard mirrored sunglasses that can make even the slightest of officer look hot as hell. The shirt on him had to be a special tailor fit. Hugged his chest like icing on a cake, and tapered down to where there was no, absolutely no extra fabric at the waist! His whole body did look like some bronze statue out in a state park. Only difference was, this one moved, and shit did it move! Every muscle in it showed when it moved!

His companion, a younger man of about 25 or 26 years old, a slightly smaller body, weighing in at about 180 pounds, but, none the less, —hot as hell looking himself, supported a chest of about 44 inches and a waist of only about 31 or 32 inches. His five foot eleven structure was supported with long legs to die for, dressed in skin hugging 501's, that damn near, —looked painted on! Especially in the bulging crotch area! Long legs that any man would love to have wrapped around himself during some good, hot, sex!

Obviously the officer was dressed in his damn hot looking, skin and muscle hugging patrol stretch pants and shirt, and of course the arms were pushing the limits on the strength of the shirt material, every time Office Hudson so much as folded his arm up even so little! Shawn pondered, "Just how in the hell did that fabric keep from ripping every time it got stretched so much by those arms?"

Shawn looked just as hot! As hot as a truly hot looking well structured man can look, to a woman, to a gay guy, and even to those guys that are not gay, but still admire and secretly drool over the sight of a male body that they envy and admire, —but in a much more secret, civilian way. He had on a simple white, nipple hugging, sleeveless, T-shirt, and a pair of 501's that most individuals would swear had to have been specially cut for him. Not one square inch of fabric in those 501's missed touching some hotter than hell part of his crotch, ass, or down the full length of his long legs. The front of those 501's simply had to have had some extra fabric added, just in the right spot, to support the extra dimension that stood out a little farther then the rest of the jeans, and of course did extend down the right leg for a very pleasant viewing experience. A very drooling viewing experience!

"Shawn, I've got a deal for you, if you're interested!" Officer Greg said to Shawn as they walked away from the garage area.

"A deal? What kind of a deal? What do you mean?"

"Shawn, I didn't need to stop our there on the highway when I saw you standing there beside your car. I was on patrol, not service duty. I could have simply driven by, you know?"

Shawn looked over toward Officer Greg and just replied with a "Yeah."

Officer Greg looked over toward Shawn, then very animatedly looked down at Shawn's crotch in such a fashion that Shawn simply could not misunderstand what the officer had just done! He made a major event out of removing his sun glasses and looking down at Shawn's big, lusty, bulge. He wanted Shawn to know that he was not "kind of looking" but was rather admiring it to its fullest, and from the length of it showing through those 501's, to its greatest extent!

Shawn looked down at his own crotch for just a second, then very quickly looked over at the officer and without saying anything, put a complete look of question on his face. He thought he liked what was happening, but he was completely confused, and had to admit it!

"Shawn, I'm married, to a woman, but I'm horny for guys all of the time. Shawn I go for guys just as often as I can, and when I saw you today, even before I saw that big crotch of yours standing out there, I knew I had to have you! I saw those damned tight 501's hugging your ass and I got all hot! Now, all I can do is hope that you will let me play with you. When I stopped at your car, I was, of course, hoping you were a gay guy, like I do every time I see some hot guy, but I didn't know for sure until I mentioned my wife and kids, and then you mentioned your man, Rog. Right then I secretly said, 'Thank you God, Thanks!' Shawn, my wife doesn't know that I play with guys, so I always have to find some way, whenever possible to make it happen, and right now I'm really begging you to say that you will! Shawn, I'll put you up, and pay for a motel room for you for the night, if you'll agree to let me come over a little later and let me fuck you. I love to fuck a guy's good tight ass, and from what I can already see, I really, really, want that one! That ass looks so damn good to me. Those Levi's are hugging that ass, and I wanna do some hugging on it too! What do you say? Interested? I'll get you a good room down at the lake resort if you'll let me come over and fuck you! I really wanna use your ass for some good hot fucking! Man, I need that ass! I really do! OK?"

"God Officer, —shit, I never expected anything like this to happen! Sir, I mean, Greg, —oh, now I understand! Yeah, —earlier you asked me to not call you Sir! You told me that kind of made you start loosing it when someone called you that! Now I understand! You like to be called Sir when you are having gay sex, right? That's why calling you Sir was getting you all shook up, isn't it?"

"Yeah, Shawn, yeah! Shawn, I like to have some good strong active male sex and I really get turned on when my man keeps calling me Sir. Shawn, please do tell me that you will agree to this. Shawn, I really do want to fuck you badly. I want to fuck your ass! Can I please? May I, please!?"

"Yes, hell yes! Any hot looking cop that looks like you do and are as horny for some guy's ass as you must be, of course you can! Hell yes! I don't usually get fucked, —I'm usually the fucker but hey, switching things around once in awhile can be OK. Hell yeah! Yeah, you can fuck me!"

Shawn then quickly looked around to make sure nobody was within eyesight of them, and after verifying that they were quite well hidden among the trees, he reached over and took hold of Greg's crotch.

"Oh shit man! Hell yes, man! Of course you can fuck me with that damn thing! Shit Greg, how damn big is that?" Shawn asked as he grabbed and then squeezed on Greg's crotch.

"It's big enough to make most of my bottom boys happy, and if you don't usually get fucked, man I'm really looking forward to putting it up in your ass, then! Shawn, it is big enough that if your ass hasn't been opened up lately, we will need to take it kind of slow until we get you opened up. OK? Still game?"

"Fuck, shit yes I am!" Shawn excitedly exploded. "Greg, what's the deal? When? Where? Greg, how soon can we do it? My God man, I had no idea you were hiding so damn much in there. You got one hell of a nice bulge showing in those pants, but how in the hell do you keep that thing from showing all of it in your uniform pants? My God Greg, you feel like you are really hung! Shit yes, I want that damn thing pushed up in my ass! I guess maybe after I get to my room, I'd better start pulling my ass open with my fingers or sit on a bed post or something, so I can try and get my ass opened up some so I can get that damn thing up in me! Shit Greg, how soon? Oh God Greg! You've got me so fucking turned on now, I'm going crazy! I wannna strip my pants off of myself right here and now, and let you push that damn thing up in me! Like I said, I don't usually get fucked, but man, I'm fucking ready for that thing right here and now! Shit man! God it feels so good! Yeah man, —I want that up in my ass! Hell yes I do! Damn I wish we could do it now! Right now!"

"Hey Shawn, let's go back to the garage and get the car and then I'll take you over and get you a room. I'll be off duty right about 8:00 and so I should be back to your room by about 8:30 or so. I'll make some excuse of why I've got to be gone from the house for the night, and maybe if things go right, I might be able to stay the whole night if you want."

"Fuck man! From what I've felt in there, the whole night might not be long enough. Shit man, it might take me half of the night to just get it up in me! Hey, Greg, what do we tell the guys at the garage. Won't they wonder just what in the hell is going on? How do we explain this to them?"

"Hey Shawn, we don't need to do any explaining at all. Jay and George have known about my guy fucking for years now, and although they sure are not part of it, they kind of help me out by helping me get things set up once in awhile. When I called them from out in the country, I told Jay that I was kind of hoping maybe you were a possible hit and so he knew from the beginning that I wanted you if possible! Jay and George have always kind of found it exciting to try and help me get a guy whenever possible, so they have no problem with it. I tried to get them to do something with me once, but other than sucking Jay off once, we've never done anything else together. I saw George really look at my dick once when I was taking a piss out in the woods once, and I asked him if he wanted it, but he said, "Hell No!" I really did think he was maybe thinking about it, but he never agreed to anything, so I quit trying! That's OK, I guess. At least they help me get stuff set up whenever possible, and I appreciate that! I kind of think they feel like they are doing some "no, no" stuff and it kind of gives them a hit to help me out when I'm being a bad guy!"

Realizing that they were well hidden from view, Shawn continued to feel, rub and squeeze the big dick that he knew would soon be going up in his ass, and Greg had both hands wrapped around Shawn's waist and was giving Shawn's tight ass a good warm-up massage, even though he could not slide his fingers up in between those cheek muscles, —just yet.

"Oh Shawn, that ass of yours feels like it is going to be one hot bucket of honey to slide my rod up into. Damn man, your ass feels solid! Solid and tight! Damn, I'm getting really, really damn anxious!"

"Greg, I'm still kind of confused about Jay and George. Are they married guys? Do they have families? They just kind of help their buddy get together with guys, even though they are straight guys?"

"Yeah! Shawn, let's face it. I gave them some business by suggesting you bring your car in here, didn't I? So, it's kind of a trade off. Of course most of the business I send them aren't gay guys, but the once in awhile, is still a good pay back for them to help me. They of course know I'm a married daddy, and they know I have to be real careful in finding and getting some guy that I can stick my dick up in, so I trust them, and we have a good friendship. Whenever it works out for me, they always congratulate me! They always act like they are happy it worked out."

Shawn and Greg took advantage of their rather hidden wooded spot and enjoyed the feel of each other and those areas of another person's body that most individuals do not usually get to fell and rub, —when things are on the rather more 'normal' standard. As they enjoyed the more masculine parts of each other's bodies, Shawn did tell Greg about the conversation that he and Jay had shared on their drive back to the garage. Greg did admit that Jay was then attempting to find out any information about Shawn's possible agreement or possible disagreement of this type of a situation. He informed Greg before Greg got to the garage that he felt that Shawn was definitely a good possible subject for Greg, and that he didn't think Greg had any reason to shy away, from just out and out asking Shawn for a chance to get in his ass. Greg explained that was why he made the approach so straight forward and quickly as soon as he got back to the garage. Jay had pretty well checked out Shawn's attitude and he had told Greg he thought Shawn would definitely be a good grab.

Greg then slapped Shawn on the ass a couple of good whacks and added, "And from what I can feel through those tight 501's, I think you are definitely going to be one hell of a good grab!"

"So does this really mean that my car doesn't really need to be here over night? Is that part of the ploy for you to get in my butt?"

"No, no!" Greg quickly answered. "No, we don't do that! No, Jay said you really do need a fuel pump, and he can't get it till tomorrow. No, if they could have gotten your car ready today, they would have. If that had been the situation, then I would have just had to tell you that I wanted to play with you and just see what you would have said. I would have just prayed that you were real horny for some good ass play, but hey, as far as I'm concerned, you having to stay here over night really is a hell of a lot better. Well, for me anyway!"

"Yeah, —for me too from what I've been feeling and rubbing on here! Man, this has made my ass hungry, real hungry! Puts me a little behind schedule from what I had planned, but shit man, getting to play with that damn big thing, it'll be worth it! You like to get it sucked on too? Will I get to suck on it, too? You gonna ram it down my throat?"

Greg looked over at Shawn, smiled, and then just said, "Tonight, tonight you'll find out! OK? Tonight!"

Officer Greg and Shawn finally let loose of each other and returned back to the garage. Greg told Jay and George that he "needed to take Shawn over to the resort and get him a room for the night," and after some rather goofing around type of laughter, Shawn grabbed an overnight bag out of his car and he and Greg headed out for the resort.

As they drove away from the garage, Greg did comment on how Jay and George were definitely in step with the success of their little "walk and talk", and did explain to Shawn that what they referred to as the "resort," was not actually on the true standard of a classy resort, but rather a cluster of small shops and motel rooms that were over along the old highway. Business had passed them by when the new highway went in, and every item of business was a very welcome bite to each proprietor.

"Greg, won't they wonder about you bringing some guy here and getting him a room? Do these people know you?"

"Hey don't worry Shawn. Once again, any business that comes in, is welcome business. They know they are not in any position to ask any questions. I always just tell them that whoever I have with me was stranded and I was just helping them out till they can get out of town the next day. Besides, they just know me as an Officer and they don't know anything else about me. See, I live over in Bellmount. Only time I'm over here is for my occasions when I need to help some guy out, if you get my gist! I'm sure they have more gals bring some guys in here for some rather short visits, than they do have me bring guys by, so I'm sure that if they do have any idea, they just keep it to themselves. But damn it, they did have one hot desk clerk here for a few months that I was always hoping would say something to me about what I was up to. Damn, I really wanted that ass! I almost suggested that he and I try out one of the rooms, but then thought I'd get a better chance sometime! But, never did! Damn it! Wish I knew where he went to!"

Greg pointed out a restaurant that was rather close to the motel and he suggested that Shawn might wish to visit, to grab some supper in, and he then pulled into the motel property and went inside of the office. He returned to the car, and then moved it to the end unit. As he parked the car, he looked at Shawn and said, "I always want an end room just incase there happens to be any yelling or screaming going on during the night. This motel is never full enough to have somebody in the room beside you, so the end rooms are always a guarantee of solitude. Works out pretty well! Especially did one particular night about a year ago! Damn I'm glad we had an end room that night!"

Greg quickly made that statement and then immediately got out of the cruiser before Shawn had any time to react or ask questions. As Shawn got out of his side of the car, he looked at Greg with somewhat of a quizzed look on his face, then changed it into a big grin, letting Greg know that whatever he had been referring to, it was really quite OK with him.

Both men approached the motel room door, and as Greg opened it with the room key which he still had in his pocket, he looked at Shawn, extended his hand for Shawn to enter the room, and said, "Hey sweet young little tight ass, —enter our playroom!"

Shawn grinned and as he walked past Greg, he very sneakingly let his hand reach out and quickly grab his officer's crotch. "Yes Sir, yes Sir!" He replied as he stepped past and gained a very quick handful of the officer's rod.

"Hey tight little ass, —I really do need to get back on duty, but I'll be here about 8:30 and you be ready for getting one hot juicy stiff dick put up in that ass of yours. OK? It's going to be a good stiff police baton, but it sure ain't gonna to be the one that I hang on my belt loop! I'm real ass fucking horny and I haven't had any guy's tight little ass for about three weeks now, so you better make sure your ass is good and ready. You're gonna be my boy tonight, and I'm gonna be your Sir!"

CHAPTER TWO:

In the Motel Room

Taking advantage of their privacy, being in the motel room, and before he hit the road to finish his day of "road duty," Greg made sure he knew just how good Shawn's ass felt, and once again reconfirmed, with his soon to be "bottom boy", that he would be back right at about 8:30 and once again instructed Shawn to be good and ready to get a good ass fucking by one hot, hung, and horny cop.

"Your ass feels damn good, and I am getting real anxious to stuff it full with my meat. You make sure you are good and ready for me when I get back, OK?"

Shawn told Greg that he sure didn't need to be reminded any more to be ready! He was already more than ready, and made one last strong grab onto the meaty steak rod that he was now really getting very, very anxious to get uncovered, get it good and hard, and to get it up and into his butt hole.

Greg slightly slapped his "bottom boy" on the ass and left to finish his day of traffic duty.

Shawn called his man Rog and told Rog of what was going on. "Yeah, I know honey, but he's just a married guy that likes to fuck a guy's ass once in awhile, and besides he's a Highway Patrolman. How wild can a guy like that be? Hey Rog Hon, if you could see the body on this guy, you'd be spreading your legs wide open for him too. Hot, —damn hot man! Hey Rog, I love you man, but I got to admit that this guy is pure prime meat as far as his body is concerned, and besides, even though I haven't seen it yet, —but I sure have grabbed it, —I kind of think that dick just might be the dick of death! Rog, he is one of those hot looking cops that we see out on the highway with those ass hugging tight, tight uniform pants on that shows every muscle he's got, and showing off his crotch like some lit up Christmas tree. Rog, I'm serious, I've gotta do it with him. I've always wanted a chance to get to one of these officers, and this one is hotter than any of 'em I've ever seen before. His shirt is so fucking tight on his big arms and his chest, I just wanna run my tongue all over it and suck on his tits through it! Rog, he is hot, fucking hot! But Rog, I'm sure he'll probably only be here long enough to get his rocks off and then hit the road. I'm sure he's so used to being drooled all over. I'm sure he's just gonna be here long enough to get his rocks off, satisfy himself and his dick, and then hit the road. I'm sure every guy that he's ever had in bed has worshiped him and his muscles, got their ass fucked, and then watched him walk out the door as the poor bottom guy just laid there and still felt horny ass hell! Hey, after he leaves, I'll probably have to jerk myself off to get my jollies for the night! Hey, I might be left just laying there feeling horny as hell, but man, I know I will have been fucked by one hell of a hot and big muscled highway officer. Rog, this is a once in a lifetime chance, and I've gotta do it. How many times have I looked at one of those guys, straddling his big hog bike, with his crotch being pushed right down tight on the gas tank, and I told you how I wanted to let him fuck the hell out of me? And besides, I'm getting a free room to use for the night while the car is out of commission. I'll be home tomorrow just as soon as they get the car fixed and I can get back on the road. Yeah, love you too. Talk to you tomorrow and I'll let you know how the fucking went! Yeah, bye honey!"

Shawn took advantage of the shower and then redressed and headed down the street to the restaurant that Greg had mentioned to him. Following a rather boring and lonesome hamburger and fries, Shawn headed back to the motel room and pondered just how he was going to spend the next two hours waiting on the magic 8:30 to arrive, and his hot looking fucking officer to arrive along with it.

As Shawn got back to the motel room, he opened the door, entered and as he closed the door he realized that there was a brown paper bag sitting on the dresser that had not been there when he left. Going over to the bag, he unfolded the top and looked in to find a note inside. "Used the other room key and left this here for you while you were out. The douche hose fits the shower head in the motel, and the grease will definitely help you out when it's, "slam it up in your ass time." So have your ass good and cleaned out and then well greased up by the time I get there! Put the candle in an ash tray and light it. See you at 8:30. Be ready boy! I need ass!"

Shawn was quite shocked, but at the same time quite pleased that Greg was showing he knew the "tricks of the game" so to say. Suddenly Shawn started to realize that Officer Greg just might have a little more gay experience than he had originally thought! He gave Rog one more quick phone call and told him about the surprise package that Greg had dropped off, and his heightened excitement that just maybe Greg was not quite the novice at this as he had assumed he was. He said he sure was glad Greg thought of some grease since he wasn't too experienced at getting it up in the ass, but the candle was a little confusing to him. He told Rog he guessed that was just so they would have some light in the room, but could have the room lights off. He told Rog he would give him a full report later, after Greg had left.

The remaining two hours passed by much more quickly for Shawn than he had originally thought it might. Part of the time was consumed with his getting the douche hose hooked up and then properly used. He grinned as he opened the small can of Crisco and imagined the Highway Patrolman going into a grocery store, all decked out in his officer's uniform and purchasing just one small can of Crisco. Shawn wondered if the grocery checkout person maybe silently wondered just why, all of a sudden this, on duty officer, just had to have a can of Crisco. And he wondered, almost out loud, just where Greg hid that shower douche hose. Unless it was in the patrol car, maybe Jay and George helped out there too.

With only two minutes to go before the magic 8:30 arrived, the room phone rang. Shawn answered it. It was Greg calling. "Hey boy, I will be there in just about 5 minutes. Did you find the hose and the grease?"

"Yeah. Yes, I did!"

"Did you use the hose?"

"Yeah Greg, yeah I did."

"Sir! Sir! Hey boy, did you hear those words? Sir! From right now on, I am Sir! Understand?"

"Uh, yeah! Yes, I do, —Sir!" Shawn responded in a rather meek and mellow shocked manner.

"OK boy, —is your ass full of grease? Did you use the grease up in there so I don't pull your innards out of you? Did you pack your ass?"

"Yes, I did. Yes, I'm all greased up, —Sir!"

"Fine. I'll be there very shortly. Have the window drapes closed, the room lights off, light the candle, and have the front door standing open. I'll be in my truck and will be parking right in front of your room! You ready for me, boy?"

"Uh, — yes, yes I am! Yes Sir, yes,—I am ready! Yes, I am ready!!"

Suddenly and with some surprise even to himself, Shawn had suddenly gained some more masculine composure and had moved beyond his state of shock with Greg's new tougher and rougher manner that he was now using.

Shawn turned off the room lights, lit the candle, opened the door and then stood back so that he was not immediately visible if, in the rare chance, anybody happened to walk past the open door. As he stood back in the shadows he watched for a truck to enter the parking lot. Within only about two minutes a very beefy extended cab Dodge Ram drove in, backed in toward his door, and to his complete surprise Greg got out, dressed only in tight leather chaps, boots, hat, arm bands, and a vest. No pants! Chaps and a completely exposed rod, swinging free, and a totally bare ass! No pants!

"Oh my God!" Shawn exclaimed to himself five times very rapidly. "Oh shit man, oh God!"

Greg entered the room, closed the door and without saying a word, swung Shawn around so that he was reaching around to the front of Shawn, and placed a leather blindfold on Shawn's face.

"There boy! There! I'll let you look at me later. Right now you just put your bare assed little body down there on that bed and I'll be right back."

Shawn heard Greg open the room door and then very quickly heard him come back into the room and close the door. He heard Greg set something onto the dresser. Then he heard the sounds of items being moved around that he was not too certain of what they were. Chains, —he heard chains! Something sounded like wood but he just was not sure! Silently he laid there, his gut down and his bare, greased, ass up pointing toward the sky, wondering just what was happening that he was not aware of.

"You trust me boy?" Greg asked. "You trust me?"

Not as totally confident as he would have answered only about 5 minutes ago, Shawn did reply, "Yeah. Yeah, —I do, —Sir."

Shawn was very quickly realizing that his previous conversation with Rog was turning out to be completely incorrect. He was now quickly becoming aware that Greg was not just the, "married daddy type" that likes to fuck some guy's ass once in awhile. He was now finding out very solidly how much more experienced and how much more sexually active Greg was, than just being the "married daddy type" of a guy. He heard the chains again.

"Last chance to change your mind boy, you trust me boy?"

Slowly and very hesitantly, and only after taking a very deep breath, Shawn did answer, "Yes sir, yes I do!"

Suddenly, very suddenly, Shawn simply knew that he was truly now the "Boy," and the big officer was the "Sir," and the actions that were going to happen from this point on were now at Greg's complete control. He realized that he had submitted his complete existence to the big man when he once again confirmed, even though very weakly confirmed, that yes he did trust him.

Shawn felt Greg grab hold of his left wrist and pull it up toward the head of the bed, and then, with somewhat of a bit of concern and some alarm, he felt Greg strapping a very heavy leather wrist strap onto that wrist. He also again heard chains.

Greg buckled the wrist restraint and then again asked, "You trust me boy? You trust me?"

Shawn seriously listened to the question and took a moment to answer. For a slight moment he thought maybe he really should admit that maybe, just maybe, he did not completely trust Greg,— now that things had changed so drastically, but he then realized that for one time in his life, he was being given the opportunity to submit himself to some other guy, somebody that was one of the hottest looking and walking human male specimen he had ever been close to, and somebody that, he now knew, must have had more experience in some wilder gay sex than he did, although he always thought that he was pretty well experienced, himself. He quickly questioned the funny little old motel that he was in, not one of the greatest places on earth, nobody else was within yelling distance that he knew about, and what if this guy just had his fun and then left him there, all chained to the bed and simply drove away. Shawn quickly attempted to analyze his safety or possibly his position of real danger. He ran so many thoughts through his mind, back and forth. One second he wanted to call everything off, just to make sure he would stay safe and unhurt, and then one second later he liked the thrill of not really knowing what was going to happen, and what was this hunk of a guy going to expect him to do. He realized that he liked the feeling of complete submission to the unknown and his feeling of letting another man, a very hot looking man, a much more muscular man, take over complete control. Mind and body, he was getting very excited at the very risky prospects, but then also, the possible factors that this could actually be one hell of a lot of wild unexpected fun, beyond his greatest beliefs. The excitement out-ruled the safety factor. He knew he had called Rog, and if anything funny did happen, at least Rog knew what town he was in, and that he was in some old motel. Which one, he had not told Rog, but at least Rog knew which town he was in.

Not getting an answer quite as quickly as Greg had wanted, he then said, "Boy, it's either you completely trust me, you turn yourself over to me for as long as we are together, you let me have my fun with you and probably teach you some new fun stuff, or you tell me right now to let you up and to stop everything. If so, then I just walk out of here and drive away. I can't tell you to trust me! Only you can decide that! All I can tell you is that if you don't trust me, you just might be missing out on the best experiences of your life! You decide! I'm into a little more than just fuck some cute little tight bare ass, but I don't play with babies. Only with boys that know how to lay their trust on the line. You trust me boy? You trust me?"

Slowly, very slowly Shawn finally managed a less than strong "Yes. Yes I do."

Immediately he questioned his sanity and then his safety. He knew he had said "yes", and he knew that with a man like Greg, and in a situation like this, you can not change your mind. Shawn knew he had just turned his complete existence and safety or lack of it, over to a man that he really did not know. Shawn realized that if any person wanted to do funny and dangerous stuff to some other guy, Greg certainly was the kind of a guy that could do it. The mere sight of the man, made possible for him, whatever he wanted to do.

Shawn suddenly realized that if Greg was not so damn hot looking, that in reality, he might never had agreed to this "deal". He realized that Greg's muscular tight form, his tight assed uniform pants, his sleeve busting biceps and his skin tight uniform pants stretching down his muscular legs, were what had made him agree to this get together. He wondered for just a second of two if maybe he could end up as the front page news story tomorrow, if this guy was way different than what he looked like. He realized weird things have happened, but he just never, ever though that maybe he would ever be in a situation to wonder if it could happen to himself. Suddenly he even wondered about Greg's friendship with Jay and George. If anything funny was happening, were they possibly part of it? Had he heard or read anything coming from this area of the country where funny things had happened to some guy, and nobody knew what the total story was.

"Good boy! Good!" Greg replied to the, "Yes, —I do!" statement.

Greg took hold of the end of the chain, and Shawn could hear it being wrapped around part of the bed frame and an actual pad lock being snapped closed on it. The left wrist was now firmly locked in place. Greg now secured the right wrist. Wrist restraint, chain and of course the pad lock. Both arms were now reaching to their limits, left to the upper left, and right to the upper right.

Shawn could feel Greg moving around the edge of the bed, but of course could not see anything due to the very effective blindfold that Greg had placed on Shawn's face. Shawn laid there and listened.

"More chains!"

Shawn's left ankle was pulled to the side, and once again a restraint and then the sound of the chain and the padlock. Shawn's right ankle was identically secured. He was now stretched in a four point across the bed. This was the very first time that Shawn had ever felt this unbelievable sense of total body exposure and total submission. Other than to turn his head back and forth, he had no control over his position, —his completely exposed position. Suddenly he realized that his ass was as if it had been positioned on the top of a coffee table, sitting there for all to see, and for all to do whatever they wished with. He had never felt his ass being quite so completely exposed before. He knew it was only he and Greg in the room, but having his ass so predominately displayed, and his inability to even cover it if he so wanted, made Shawn have raging surges of sexual energy that he had never felt before. He, being blindfolded, could not see anything, yet he knew that the one major part of him that was so completely standing out, was his bare ass. Never had he ever been in a position where his bare ass was the only point of interest to be showing!

Never had Shawn been in a position of being completely bare assed exposed, restrained so that he could not move nor have any body movements, and also be completely blinded so that he could not have the slightest of hint about what might be happening next. His mind kept flipping back and forth from fear and possible fright to the sexy, manly, wild animal serge of do it,— do it, —do it to me, I can do it, I can take it! He even thought of the idea that he was now locked into a position, where a whole line of people could come through the room, if someone wanted to do that to him, and look at his bare ass, and he could do nothing about it. He truly knew he had never, in his entire life, ever submitted himself, so completely and totally, to such an un-self-controlled position.

The silence in the room when Greg was not walking around was mystical. Shawn would listen to this left and then to his right, attempting to find some kind of a hint as to what the man that now owned his body was going to do next.

Quietly Shawn laid there and listened. He heard the snap of plastic, or so he thought. "Yes," he thought to himself. "That was a glove he heard snap on. Greg is putting on surgical gloves! Oh shit man! Oh God, he's not planning on putting his fist up in me, is he? Oh God! Oh Shit man, maybe I really screwed up telling him I trusted him. Oh shit! My ass has never had anything like that pushed up in there. Oh God! Oh Shit! No, no! I can't take a hand up in my ass!"

Shawn felt Greg sit down on the side of the bed. He felt Greg's right hand lay down on his right butt cheek. As he could feel Greg re-position himself on the edge of the bed, he then felt Greg rest his left hand on his left buttock. Shawn laid there praying that his thoughts of maybe getting fisted might be all wrong. Oh God he prayed that he was over reacting.

Shawn felt Greg's hands both move so slightly and so gently as he started to feel the firmness of Shawn's muscular ass muscles, and each hand so slightly slid down into the crevasse of Shawn's ass, and so very lovingly approached the slight tight little hole that Shawn had so recently been anxious for Greg to push his rod up into, and plant it firmly, if he could even take that much up in there. Now Shawn had some very deep concerns about if he wanted anything stuffed up in there. Shawn had not originally even considered the possibility of anything other than Greg's dick being put up in there. Being chained down, and having his entire bare body exposed, and actually being offered up as a possible sacrifice, gave Shawn new reasons to question exactly what were the possibilities of actions happening to him and his body, especially his ass. Actions that he had never even considered as a possibility. He wondered if he had completely thought this entire thing through.

Slowly Greg's hands continued to massage Shawn's ass and so very lovingly kept sliding closer and closer to that cute little opening in Shawn's body that Shawn was trying to keep tightly slammed shut.

Finger one found the hole. "Oh wow!" Greg uttered as he managed to force that first finger up and into Shawn's tight ass. "Oh shit man! Damn your ass is tight boy! God Shawn, how do you ever shit man? God Shawn that little hole is so damn tight! Yeah boy, grab my finger! Yeah, grab it boy!"

Shawn was not intentionally slamming his ass tight, but as Greg's finger attempted to move on in and up in farther, Shawn's asshole automatically attempted to push that finger back out. Greg loved the feeling of that strong muscle action, and he responded by pushing even that much more forcefully.

Listening to Shawn moan and groan, Greg knew that mentally everything was quite OK. He knew that Shawn was secretly fighting an internal war. Mentally he was excited about having this action done to him, and yet mentally he was very dubious about if he should be letting this happen to his ass. Greg knew that mentally Shawn wanted to feel a lot up in his ass, but he also knew that mentally Shawn was trying to convince his body to reject anything that was being put up in there. Greg rather silently snickered at the humor of how he knew Shawn wanted it, his body wanted it, yet he mentally did not think he should be wanting it, so he was trying to tell his body to refuse anything that was not normal back there. Greg knew that being chained down in a four point removed any actual decisions that Shawn could make, other than total and complete submission, and total and complete acceptance of anything of any action that happened back there, regardless of how he did not think it should be happening to him. Greg knew that he was offering to Shawn, totally new awareness of his intellectual thinking of knowing this is all wrong, and Shawn's physical screaming for more of it, more of it, do me man, do me!

As Greg continued to massage and rub Shawn's ass, and continued to finger Shawn's tight asshole, Greg decide to have some weird fun with Shawn and asked him if he had ever had a cucumber put up in his ass.

Immediately Shawn flipped his head to the side where Greg was and almost yelled, "No! Hell no! Greg, please don't put a cucumber up in my ass! Please I'm not sure I could get it out!"

"Hey boy, I only asked. I'm not putting any cucumbers up in your ass! I just wondered if you had ever done that! I did once. Well, more than once! Found out the bigger they are, the better they feel. Felt damn good! Took a few hours before it was ready to pop back out, but hey, a guy shits them out just like shit! Just keep it whole and not broken, and your ass thinks it's a pile of shit! Ever stuck anything up in your ass before, boy?"

"No, no just a guy's dick. That's all! No, that's all. Have you stuck other stuff up in your butt beside a cucumber?"

"Oh, yeah! I guess I really like to have my ass played with. Hard bowled eggs, pealed of course, oranges, ice cubes, and oh yeah, once a pool ball. A guy bet me I couldn't, so he grabbed one off of a pool table as we walked out of the bar, and when we got to the parking lot, I dropped my pants, he put a little lube on it, and bingo—I had a pool ball up in my ass. Took it out later that night after I got home. Have no idea of what that bar figured happened to their number three ball that night!"

"Oh God Greg, ohhhhh, I mean Sir. Oh shit man that sounds so damn hot! I've never played around with my ass like that! You're not planning on putting any of that stuff up in my ass tonight are you? Sir, please don't!"

"Hey boy! Wait, I asked you if you trusted me didn't I?"

"Yeah."

"Well then, quit worrying about your little ass. I'm not going to do anything to it that I shouldn't do. Some of it you might try to beg me to not do, but hey, tonight you are my boy toy, so tonight you have some new experiences. OK?"

"Oh God yeah, I guess so! Oh Sir, remember I have not done much other than suck and get sucked, and fuck and get fucked. OK? Sir, I want to have fun and let you have fun, but please remember, I haven't done too much funny stuff. Especially with my ass!"

"Hey boy, your ass is going to be fine. Maybe a little bigger by the time we get done, but it is going to be fine."

Greg continued to play with Shawn's ass, and although he did get some groaning and some begs of please don't, Greg did manage to open Shawn's little chute enough to get a finger from both hands in and then far enough to start pulling on the sides to get it to start opening up some. Greg could tell from the reactions, this action on his ass was something rather new to Shawn.

"Never had a guy pull your ass open before?" He asked Shawn as he managed to slightly open it ever so slowly.

"No! No I've never had a guy pulling on it like that! Remember, I told you this afternoon that I'm almost always top when I have sex. I hardly ever get my ass played with. Rog is really a total bottom, so it's always me on top of him."

"Have you ever used a dildo on yourself?"

"Yeah, I have a couple of times, but that's been a long time ago. I guess you can pretty well say I've got a pretty virgin ass. But Sir, I'm not complaining about how you are making it feel now. When you first got your fingers up in there, it hurt, but now it's feeling pretty good, so if you want to pull it open more, I'll try to just keep my mouth shut and let you do it. OK?"

"Hey great boy! That's good! See I knew that if you just kind of hung in there with me, that you'd be glad. So my fingers are starting to feel good, uh?"

"Yeah. Yes they are Sir." Shawn gave Greg some ass movement as he made this reply, which of course did indicate to Greg that Shawn was expressing that if a little bit of finger is good, them maybe a lot of finger is better. His ass was expressing hunger. Greg took advantage of that. He allowed the two fingers that he had up in Shawn's ass to reach in farther, and at the same time he also introduced two more fingers. Shawn jerked and groaned, but then relaxed back down as an indication of, "OK, do me!"

First the one finger, then the two and finally having four fingers up in Shawn's ass was making progress. The four fingers worked as an orchestrated internal lever to force the sides of Shawn's tight ass to loosen up and start opening up. Greg was having a great time playing with Shawn's asshole, and he found it to be quite exciting each little bit that he managed to pry open.

Positioning himself so that his face was up close to where his fingers were doing their deed, Greg then leaned forward and let his tongue slip out and so very gently and very lovingly slightly lick on the edge of Shawn's ass. This slight touch created a great response from Shawn.

"Oh my God Sir, Oh I can feel that! Oh Sir, lick my ass some more please! Oh God that feels so damn good! Oh, God that feels good!"

Greg was kind of taken back with Shawn's explosive reaction to feeling his ass so slightly getting touched by Greg's tongue and he then leaned back a little and asked. "Boy haven't you ever had your ass licked before? Is this the first time you've ever had your asshole licked on?"

"Yeah Sir, yeah. I've never had someone lick on me there. Oh yeah Sir that feels so damn good, oh please keep it up!"

Greg intensified his licking efforts since he had just found out that he was on a more virgin ass that he had assumed. He knew Shawn had hardly ever been fucked before, but he sure did assume that he had at least been licked clean back there before.

After quite an extended time of using his tongue on Shawn's ass, Greg repositioned himself and started getting himself in position for some good ass fucking.

Keeping his skin tight leather chaps on, and just using his rod from its open front position, Greg raised himself up high enough to aim his nine inch stiff rod right at Shawn's ass and then told Shawn, "Hang on boy, I'm about ready to fuck you and fuck you good!"

Then reaching over to the bed stand, Greg grabbed Shawn's cell phone and asked Shawn what Roger's phone number was. Shawn tried to look back at Greg as if to ask why, but he really was not in any position to do that, and Greg just said, "Hey, just tell me his number. I want you to be on the phone with him when I go up into your ass. What's his number?"

Shawn told Greg, Roger's number, and Greg dialed it. He then laid the phone down on the mattress so that Shawn could talk into it and hear from it.

As the phone was answered on the other end, Shawn said, "Roger, this is Shawn. Roger, Greg wants me to be on the phone with you while he fucks my ass. Yeah—yeah, but Hon, I'm all tied down. Both of my wrists are tied down and so are my ankles. Greg dialed the phone and then laid it down here so I could talk to you—Oh shit!! Oh God man, Oh, —Rog he is starting to fuck me! Oh God Rog!! Oh Rog his dick feels so damn big!! No, I don't know!

As soon as he got here he blindfolded me and told me I could see it later. No, I've been blindfolded ever since he got here. He, —Oh God man! Oh shit! Oh God man, —he's pushing it in me! Oh Rog, you know I never get it in the ass, —oh shit man, —ouch, —oh Greg that hurts! Greg it's hurting!! Ouch, Greg my ass just can't take this, man, —it can't take it!! It must be too fucking big!"

"You're doing good Boy, you just talk to your lover boy and you tell him how it feels to get fucked, OK? You tell your honey man that you are about to feel more up in your ass than you have ever had up in there before, and after tonight you are going to want to be fucked a lot, so your man had better start fucking you more, OK?"

"Oh Roger he is still fucking me and it hurts. Oh there, —there, he pulled back some. Oh Roger his dick must be really, really big! It feels like it is so big!"

"Hey Shawn Boy, tell me what your honey man is telling you. What's Roger telling you?"

"He's telling me that everything will be OK. He's just telling me to just lay here and try to relax."

"Hey you got yourself a smart man there Boy. You tell your Roger man that your ass is getting kind of full but you're going to take it, and take it all! OK?"

"Yeah, he said he could hear you! He told me to try and relax my ass."

Then directing it to Roger, Shawn asked, "Honey, is it supposed to hurt like this or is he trying to fuck me too fast? Roger Honey, I don't remember you saying it hurts like this, —ouch, —ouch, —oh shit man! Oh Roger he just slammed my ass! Oh man, he just pushed it in all the way! Roger my ass is hurting man! Oh Roger he is really pushing on it hard in me! Oh Roger, I just took his whole dick! I can tell he's got it all up in me, I can feel his body laying on top of me! Yeah, —yeah he's just laying on me. He's got chaps and his vest on. I can feel the leather against me. It feels like I'm getting fucked buy some kind of an animal. Oh Rog, his leather has studs in it and I can feel them poking me. Yeah, —no they don't hurt. Yeah, —it's not hurting so much now. Yeah, —he's still pushing on it pretty hard, but it quit hurting now. Now it's feeling like it's OK. Yeah, it feels kind of like it's pretty normal! Yeah, he's kind of biting the back of my neck. Yeah, —yeah Rog, it feels pretty good. Hey Roger man, his dick is starting to quit hurting. Yeah, yeah it's starting to feel pretty good up in my ass! Yeah, it's kind of quit hurting! Yeah, it quit hurting! Yeah, OK, —oh shit!! Oh Rog!! Now he is really pumping my ass! Oh God man, he is really slamming my asshole now! Oh shit man he is really pumping me! Oh shit that feels good! Hey, can you hear me? I can't move the phone and I think it might have moved. Yeah, my hands are still tied. Yeah, —he brought some leather straps that he buckled on me and then locked some chains onto the bed frame. Yeah, —my wrists and my ankles. Yeah, —I can't move. My ass is about the only part not tied down, and he's laying on it with his big dick all the way up in me. Oh Rog Hon, —he is really fucking the hell out of me right now! He is fucking me hard as hell right now! Yeah, —Rog, he's going to make a baby in me the way he is fucking me man! Oh Rog, honey, —I've got to admit this is feeling really pretty good! Oh, I've never had a guy fuck me like this! Oh Rog, I love getting fucked like this man, I do! Oh shit man, he is really pounding my ass! Oh my God Rog! If he cums while he is fucking me like this he will blow my brains out! Oh shit man, I'll be so full of cum if he cums in me! God Roger, he is fucking me so fucking hard! Oh my ass!! Oh, don't stop man, —don't stop! Yeah man, yeah! Do it, do it!"

"Hey Boy, tell your Roger man that once you get home, you're gonna need to get your ass fucked some more! OK?"

"Hey, Rog Hon, did you hear him? He wants me to tell you that when I get home I will want my ass fucked again. And Rog Honey, I think he might be right! Roger Honey, this is feeling good! Yeah his dick is feeling good. It keeps going down in me deeper and deeper. I thought I had all of it earlier, but now I think it either got longer, or it's going in deeper. It feels like it's up in my stomach! Yeah, —no, —yeah, —it's OK. Yeah, —no, it feels good! No, it don't hurt! No, it really, really feels good now!"

All of a sudden Shawn heard the room door open and then close. He knew Greg was still fucking his ass, so he knew it had to be an additional person. The fact that Greg never stopped fucking let Shawn know that whoever it was, it was OK with Greg.

"Oh Rog, —somebody else just came in the room! Rog, somebody else just came in. Greg, who just came in the room? Who else is here?"

"Hey Shawn Boy, tell your Roger man that you've got to go for now. We have another person here that wants some of you too, so tell your Roger man that you'll call him later and tell him how everything is going. OK? Tell him Bye Bye!"

CHAPTER THREE:

But, Somebody Else Just Came In

"Hey Rog Honey. I don't know what's going on. I'm still blindfolded and I don't know who else is here, but somebody else just came in, and Greg said he wants some of me too! I don't know. Rog, I'm all chained down to the bed. All I can do is whatever Greg says. Honey, I love you, I got to go! He told me to tell you good-bye. Roger, I'll try and call later!"

With that statement, Greg reached up, took the phone and hung up.

"Hey Shawn boy, say Hi to Bill. He likes tight asses like I do, so I told him we'd be here and for him to stop in if he wanted some too."

Bill slapped Shawn on the ass and said, "Hi Boy! I'm Bill! I guess maybe we'll meet face to face later if Greg here lets you get un-blindfolded, but for now, I'll just know you as one bare assed guy that is getting fucked by his buddy Greg, and just as soon as I can get my pants down, and my dick out, by me too. You got a nice looking ass there man, and I'm all ready to use it! I got me a piece of meat here that needs a nice piece of ass, and it sure does look right now like that piece of ass is yours! Hope you like dick back there boy cause that's right where my dick is gonna go!"

"So Greg, tell me. How's this guy doing? You told me earlier on the phone, that he said that he doesn't get it up in the ass very often. He doing OK? He taking that dick of yours OK?"

"Yeah Bill, he's taking it good. He kind of screamed a little when I first punched it up in him, but he was busy talking to his lover boy on the phone then, so he kind of had his mind on other stuff."

"So how's his lover man taking it knowing that you are back there fucking his ass, and all he can do is listen about it on the phone?"

"I don't know for sure."

"Hey, Shawn Boy, —tell me and Bill what your Roger man said about me fucking your ass while he talked to you. Is this all OK with him? What did he say?"

Shawn had been laying there, continuing to get fucked, as Greg and Bill talked about him, but he had not attempted to say anything.

Shawn then answered Greg's question. "Oh he just kind of wanted to know what was happening, and I just told him I was getting fucked by you and your obviously very big dick. He just told me to play along and don't try to fight back any, and he thought everything would probably be OK. He said it sounded kind of like Greg was just into some good playing and not into anything dangerous, so he told me to just play along. When he found out some other guy had just come in though, he did say, 'Oh shit,' just before he hung up. He might be a little worried about me now. I am OK yet ain't I guys? I mean, nothing is going on kinda funny here is it? I really kinda do like the idea of two of you guys using me, but I'm still OK, ain't I?"

"Hell yeah Boy! You're still alright!" Greg replied.

"Hey Bill, you about ready to take over here shortly?" Greg asked.

"I'm ready to punch that cute little ass whenever you want to pull out of it! I need to do some fucking, and that ass looks good and sweet to me right now! I ain't had me no man ass for too long now, and I'm ready! Thank goodness you called me and told me you were getting some ass tonight!" Bill said.

"OK, let's change. I'm going to go in and wash the grease off of it and then let my Boy find out, in his mouth, and down in his throat just what he's had up in his ass. I got him blind folded just as soon as I got here, so all he saw was it hanging kind of limp, so now I want him to see how much dick he can take down that throat of his while he takes all of your big dick up in his ass. He's got a good tight ass, so you're really gonna enjoy poking it man! It'll grab ahold of that dick of yours and make it feel like you've got it stuck in some kinda vice grip!"

"Hey Shawn Boy," Greg said. "If you think your ass was kind of full with my dick, just you wait until big Bill slams his dick up in you, —but he's not gonna start fucking you until I get my dick in your mouth, so you can't scream out too loud! When that dick goes up in you, I know you're gonna wanna scream like some old railroad loco just drove right up in you! This is what we like to refer to as making our sandwich. Bill's on one side, I'm on the other, and you certainly are the piece of meat between the two of us! Hang tight guys, I'll be right back."

Greg got up from the bed and headed for the bathroom.

Bill sat down on the side of the bed and started rubbing Shawn's ass. "Oh yeah man! Yeah, this ass is going to feel good on my dick! Real good!"

Waiting for Greg to return from the bathroom, Bill took advantage of the time to finger Shawn's ass first with one finger, then very quickly two fingers, and then immediately three fingers. Shawn accepted the ass play with pleasure and constantly kept saying, "Oh yes Sir! Oh yes! That feels so damn good! Oh finger me man, finger me!"

Greg finished in the bathroom and rather quickly returned back into the room, positioned himself at the head of the bed, spread his legs on each side of Shawn's face, pointed his dick down toward Shawn's face and said, "Open up hungry guy! Open up! You've got a hotdog to eat here, and it's real ready for some tongue licking and some throat sucking on it! It's stiff and ready for you to take care of it man!"

Shawn agreeably raised his face up, opened his mouth, and said, "Yeah, oh yeah!" Greg could tell his Shawn Boy was real ready for taking in some good mouth fucking. He knew he was anxious and was not going to object to this! He knew his dick had felt good up in Shawn's ass, and he was damn sure it was gonna feel just as good getting rammed down his throat.

Greg took hold of his nine inch rod and moved it into Shawn's mouth. "Open up your throat man, I'm pushing it in! It's pay dirt time man, it's pay dirt time!"

Shawn was glad Greg had given him a slight warning since all of a sudden he had a complete mouth and throat full! Greg had taken hold of Shawn's head and had rammed his dick into Shawn's mouth faster then he had fucked his ass. With one quick thrust, his entire rod was fully and completely imbedded into Shawn's mouth! Shawn chocked and gagged, but he took it gladly! He wanted to be able to reach over and grab Greg by the hips and pull him up even closer so he could take more dick, if there was anymore to take, but his hands were tied and he had to be satisfied with the nine inches that he did have in there to suck and swallow on as much as he could!

"OK Bill!" Greg said as he took hold of the back of Shawn's head and forced his dick down into Shawn's throat. "I've got his mouth full, fill his ass man, fill his ass!"

Bill aimed his dick, and knowing that Shawn's ass was already greased and had already been opened up quite well with Greg's nine inch rod, he immediately slammed his body down and drove his enormous dick down and into Shawn's ass.

Shawn did attempt to scream! Greg looked up at Bill and Bill looked back at Greg. Each man rather grinned at the other person. They each knew they were part of a pretty determined team in taking care of both ends of a sexually hungry man all at the same time. One hot ass, and one hot and hungry mouth! This was not the first time that one of the two had fucked a guy's face while the other man fucked his ass. And the way they did it, always created a great and strong reaction from the man that was being used on both ends. Shawn had reacted just as they had expected. He constantly tried to get more dick in his mouth, and at the same time, kept offering his anxious ass back at Bill, hoping for more and more dick. They knew Shawn was living in sexual heaven getting fucked by two hot built men, one on each end and both of 'em trying to get their dicks to meet together someplace in the middle of him.

"God man! I'm glad I had his mouth full when you did that." Greg happily said. "If you would've rammed that damn thing up in him that fast and his mouth was open and empty, half of the town would have heard him screaming. I guess that's where the saying, 'pain in the ass' comes from! You OK, Shawn? You OK?"

Shawn attempted to kind of say "Yes", and he kind of tried to slightly shake his head, but he was not able to do either. Suddenly he wondered, — what if he wasn't really OK. Both of the men assumed that he was OK, but Shawn realized that it was impossible to let them know if he was not OK. His mouth was jammed full all the way down his throat, his ass was now full of something, —what in the hell it was he really was not too sure, since he really wondered if that was all dick, and of course both of his arms and both of this legs were still chained down tight! He had totally relinquished all personal and physical control to his two fuckers, the one in his throat and the one all the way up in his ass!

Suddenly Shawn realized that his ass was getting rammed in and out of, quickly and forcefully, and the same thing was happening to his mouth. He felt like both ends of his body were being jack hammered by some big strong construction worker trying to tear up an old sidewalk! He certainly did not complain, but he certainly did realize that he had never, in his entire life enjoyed something so hot, something so radically happening to him, as he did this! He realized that on one end of his body, he had one hell of a hot looking and hot built Highway Officer fucking his mouth with every bit of gusto that he could muster, and back in his ass end, he had another guy that he hadn't even seen yet! Some guy that all he knew about was that he sure as hell knew how to fuck an ass, and he had a fucking big dick to do it with! Although he hadn't yet even seen the guy, he knew from the feel of his body touching his, and the strength that he was using on his ass, along with the rather enormous dick that he had just slammed up into him, he had to probably be as hot of a looking man as the officer that was fucking his mouth! He knew that after this was over, he would probably be stiff and sore, but allowing these two hot muscled men to use him and his body this way, was just way too hot and to damned exciting to even think it was possible! Suddenly he no longer felt like a living human being, but rather much more like a stuffed play doll that was designed for, and was supposed to always be slammed and rammed this way! Some kind of a stuffed toy that these two guys bought in a store, brought home, and were now fucking the hell out of it without any regard to how much abuse and force they were using on it! To them, he was now their toy, their sex toy!

Shawn had known for a long time that one of his most secret desires was to be sexually abused by some really hot looking man, and not have any say about what was happening to himself, but this was working out to be way more than even a deep secret desire could be. He knew he had never even admitted to his lover Roger, that he wanted to be treated and abused physically this way. He had always felt that to admit this raging desire, to any other person, was to admit some kind of a sickness. He had never allowed himself to think about this type of action in a very favorable way. He just knew that wanting to be used this way, had to be something very sick. He just knew that nobody was ever supposed to have any type of a desire to have his body so completely overtaken my some other person and so brutally use it! But now that it was actually happening, he was in heaven! His body was being slammed, rammed, shook and forced to accept dicks in both ends, at the same time, in such a fashion that it was truly impossible for him to understand that this could actually be happening. He knew he was being used like a stuffed toy. These two men were not looking at him as a human being any longer, —just some item to use and abuse to their enjoyment, —something to stick their dicks into and although he had never even pondered what that would feel like, suddenly he knew the feeling, and he did not want it to pass. He realized now what a young man, one that totally and completely turns his entire life over to a Master, must feel like. This experience was giving him feelings of total, and complete physical submission that he had never imagined. Never imagined, but suddenly and very seriously liked and loved. Suddenly he did not care if this ever stopped or not. Suddenly he did not care if he ended up rather physically abused. Suddenly he did not care if he ever went back to his normal type of living. Suddenly he did not care if this could be considered being raped. He did feel ashamed of liking what was happening to himself, if this could be considered being raped, but he was liking it! He did not want to enjoy something, that is so negative in society, to actually feel so unbelievably great to him in reality. He kept telling himself that this could not be rape, even though he could not stop it if he wanted to, because it was so exciting to him, and it really did feel so good, even though it was turning into something really kind of mean and really rough, he wanted to just think of it as great, fun, and some different stuff. He knew that as he told himself that he was really getting raped, just that thought of that word, made him want it more! He liked the idea that these two unbelievable hunks were using him for all of the hot and lustful joy they could get out of him. He knew he was being used, and he liked it! He wanted to be able to pay back to his two fuckers, something, in some way, for what he was experiencing. They were giving him feelings that he did not even know existed! He wanted to scream out loud of how great this rough fucking, in both ends felt! He wanted everybody to know that he was finally getting the rough, manly strong, sexual activities that he had so secretly dreamed of for so long! Internally he did not know the 'why', but he did know that he had been wanting to be treated this way by some big strong man, for a hell of a long time. He knew that he had tried to abuse himself sexually, in so many different ways, trying to reach this kind of an excitement, but he had never been remotely successful in reaching that goal! Now, to finally being in a situation where two unbelievable hunks of strong muscle men were completely using him, he was finally reaching that goal of just being a man's toy. He knew that he was finally being taken away from being himself and finally, after many years of wanting to feel it, he was letting himself truly become something like a rag doll. Right then, he didn't wish to be a human being, but rather an inanimate object that could almost be turned inside out, if that is what his "man" wanted to do! His dream of being used by one big strong muscle man, was now actually happening, but it was being done by two big strong muscle men. Shawn knew he was experiencing a once in a lifetime goal and action. And he knew it was something that hardly any other man in the world was ever going to get the same chance to do and live with!

From the way he was being slammed and banged, he truly did wonder if maybe these two, hot, hunks had suddenly forgotten that the thing they were each fucking was actually was another living, human being. He wondered if when this was all over, would they suddenly shake their heads and admit that they had gotten so carried away that they had each forgotten that Shawn was a live, living human being. That they had stepped out of reality for a minute or two and were thinking they were each playing with something that did not have feelings. Or, did they already know that being treated so roughly in this way, that they could transform Shawn into an unimaginable feeling that he had never experienced before, nor even imagined could be possible before? Shawn wondered if these two men had ever done any other man this same way! This unbelievably rough and rather, "out of control" way. A way he was loving! He wanted to be that man, if there had been a previous man. And if they ever did this to another man in the future, he wanted to be that man too. He begged to himself that they never stop. He wanted to be treated this way, this roughly, this physically, this abusive way, for the rest of his life. He had never felt so submissive, so helpless to any other person in his entire life, and he was overly taken, mentally, that he was allowing his entire being to be used by these two men, and one being a man that he had never even seen or met before! He knew that if they did not un-blindfold him, that man could actually get up, get dressed, and leave the room and he would never know what that person looked like. He realized that if that happened, everyday of his life from that time on, he would look at every well built man and wonder if that just happens to be the same man that fucked the hell out of him that night, in that little motel room. The same man that used his ass rougher and better than any other man had ever done!

Shawn knew he had just turned his life into something totally different than it had ever been. He was getting fucked frantically in the mouth and even more frantically in the ass, and he loved it. He had never been treated this roughly and this manly before, and he loved it. He liked the feeling that he was only a toy to them, but yet he was man enough to take whatever they dished out. He loved the fact that these two hunks of men had enough faith in him, knowing that they could get this rough with him and his body, and he would be able to take it! He knew they were not holding back from doing just what they each wanted to do, and right now, it was —doing it to him! And he loved it! He decided that he had just become sexual trash. He was being trashed, and he loved it! He wanted to submit his body to this abuse just as often as these two men wanted to abuse him. He wanted to become their permanent piece of meat. He didn't care if he ever fucked another guy, if giving that up would allow him to be treated this way forever! He mentally decided that he wanted Bill's dick up his ass forever, and Greg's dick down his throat forever!

He knew this was only gonna be happening for just a little while longer, but he wanted to have both of these hunks in him, top or bottom, forever. He decided that he was now, finally experiencing true sex, and sex the way he's always wanted it!

As Shawn offered and delivered his entire being to the two men, he could slightly hear one of the men talking to him.

"Hey Shawn, hey Shawn. You OK?"

Trying to come back to reality from his state of ecstasy and excitement, he heard Bill talking to him.

"Hey man, you got yourself a damn nice ass here, and from what I've got in my hand here, you've got one hell of a nice dick here, too! Hey Shawn boy, you wanna fuck with this thing? You ain't so badly hung yourself, you know it?! You like to fuck some guy's ass with this thing?"

As Shawn regained some normal consciousness, he then realized that Bill had reached around him, never stopping the rough house ass slamming, and had grabbed hold of his dick, and was pumping it as he fucked Shawn's ass.

"Yeah Shawn, you feel good! You got a good big dick on you boy!"

"Hey Greg, have you played with this guy's dick yet? He is damn well hung! It is one hell of a thick cock from the way it feels. Shit man, this damn thing is thick! My hand hardly reaches all the way around it! Shit man! I thought I just came here to do some hot fucking, but shit man, now that I feel that, I'm going to need to feel that thing up in my ass before the night is over. Greg, you haven't been fucked by this thing yet?"

"No Bill, I haven't even felt it out in the open yet. I really haven't even seen it yet. When I chained him down, it was soft, so no, —I haven't even seen it puffed up yet! Feels like a good one to get fucked by, uh?"

"Hell yes it is! I'd like to get double fucked by you two if you guys are up to it!" Bill exclaimed. "Hell yes! Damn I need that!"

"Shit man, it must be good if you're wanting to use it for a double fuck!" Greg exclaimed. "Shit man! It's been a long time since you've asked to be double fucked, hasn't it? I mean, maybe you've done it with somebody else, but it's been probably a year or more since you've asked me and some other guy to double fuck you. It feels that big uh?"

Shawn was laying there listening to the two men discuss Bill getting double fucked and since he had never been part of something like that, he wondered just how that could be done. He did not intend to stop anything though, to ask how that could be done. He was sure that if they wanted to do that, they would give him instructions of what to do. How, he didn't know how, but he sure did like the idea of being part of it. The whole idea of him and Greg fucking Bill's ass at the same time, — WOW! He liked that idea! Something totally different than what he had ever done before, and right now the more new and exciting things that they could teach him, the more excited he was getting! And the mere idea of watching two dicks going up in a guy's ass at the same time was really an exciting thought, and then to realize that his dick was going to be one of those two, that was simply something that was way beyond belief! He knew what it felt like to get one dick pushed up into his ass, the thought of some guy getting his ass opened up enough to take two at the same time was almost too much to even think about, and yet he was going to be one of those two dicks! Even though Bill was grabbing it and playing with it, the idea that he was gonna be part of double fucking Bill's ass, just made his dick that much more excited!

Shawn was wishing his arms were loose so he could grab around Greg and hug him while he fucked his face, but since he was still chained down to the bed, he just laid there and let the two men use him. Greg continued to forcefully fuck his face and choke his throat, and Bill continued to fuck his ass as if it was the very first ass he had ever been in before.

"Hey Bill!" Greg stated. "Tell you what lets us do. Let's unchain him, turn him over since you said he's got such a nice dick, and one of us can sit on his face and also suck on his dick, while the other guy holds his legs up in the air and fucks the hell out of his ass. What do you say?"

"Yeah, hell yeah!" Bill responded. "But I get to sit on his face and suck on that cock first. OK? I want to chew on that hunk of meat, while he swallows mine!"

"OK, sounds like a winner to me!" Greg answered.

Bill pulled out of Shawn's asshole, and Greg pulled out of his mouth.

"Hey Bill, let's leave the chains locked to the bed frame in case we want to re-lock him back up again, and just take the wrist and ankle restrains off so we can turn him over, OK?"

"Yeah, sounds good to me!" Bill answered.

The two 'tops' unbuckled Shawn and flipped him over on the bed.

"Shit man!" Greg said. "Shit man, you are right! He does have one hell of a piece of meat on him, doesn't he? Hell, now I understand why he is always top at home. Shit man! If I was his Roger, I'd be making him fuck me all the time too! Shit man! Roger should have a pretty wide open asshole, shouldn't he? God Bill! Do you think you can get my dick and his dick up in you at the same time? Look at how damn thick that thing is!"

"I sure as the hell am going to try! I haven't been double fucked for way too long now, and looking at that thing makes my ass itch for action."

Shawn had never been played with like this, being flipped over in a bed, by two hot hunky men before, and especially since he still could not see anything, he truly did feel like a rag doll. Not a person, but a stuffed doll, and especially since he was right there, but the two men were talking about him as if he was not even in the room.

"Greg, I'm serious man, I want to sit on that damn thing! Before we fuck him some more, can I sit on you and him? I really wanna feel that going up in me man! I wanna feel my ass open up for that and your dick going in with it! Man, I need that!"

"Yeah Bill, if you want to, it's OK with me."

"Hey Shawn Boy." Greg then addressed toward their anxious and hungry piece of play meat. "Bill wants to feel you and me going up in him at the same time, so what I'm gonna do is lay down here facing the opposite direction, and you and I are gonna push our crotches up together so that our dicks are right up against each other, and then Bill is gonna squat down on us and fill his ass with a couple of dicks. Understand?"

"Yeah, yeah I guess I do. So I just kind of lay here and then what? What? We intertwine our legs? Is that what you mean?"

"Yeah that's right! Here, let me put my right leg underneath your left leg, and then I'll scoot right up to where our bags are touching each other, and point our dicks up in the air and Bill'll sit right down on 'em. He might scream when he does, but he's determined that he wants both of us up in his ass at the same time, so I figure it's his asshole, not mine! If he thinks he can get it opened that far, so be it! If he can take both of ours, I'll be totally convinced that he's been putting more big stuff up in there than I ever heard about!"

"Hey Bill, you think this is going to work with me still having my chaps on? Think I need to take 'em off first?"

"No Greg, don't take them off. I want to see if we can do it with 'em on. I like the feeling of 'em when I touch you. You guys ready for me to climb up and try to get those two big sticks up inside of my ass?"

"Yeah I think we are! You ready boy?"

"Yeah, I'm ready Sir, but is it possible that maybe I could watch what is happening? I've never done this before and I'd like to watch it happen if possible! Could I maybe take this blindfold off so I can see?"

"What do you think Bill? Think we should let the boy watch what is happening?"

"Yeah I guess so Greg. If we think he needs to be blindfolded again later, we can put it back on him then."

"OK boy, take the blindfold off."

Shawn did take the blindfold off and was damn glad that they had let him do that. Finally he had a good chance to check out Greg in his stretch tight black leather chaps and he finally had a chance to check out the guy that had been fucking his asshole so wildly just a few minutes ago. Shawn had no disappointments in checking out either man! Greg had taken his vest off, and with the muscles and the form that he had, Shawn was very glad that Greg was showing it all! He remembered that he was one hot God with his uniform shirt on earlier, and when he got to the motel room, he had been blindfolded so fast that he really had not had a chance to check out Greg's body in the leather attire. He decided that it looked even better in the leather than it had earlier in the Highway Patrol uniform! Of course he did have to admit that since Greg was now showing a very strong and solid stiff nine inch cock, that just might have helped the excitement level of seeing him in the leather.

Bill's body was a lot more than Shawn had assumed when he was still blindfolded. Bill looked to Shawn to be about 40 years old, probably a good six foot tall, a very short black flat top hair cut on top of one of the squarest faces and massive necks that Shawn could remember seeing. Bill's chest, arm and back muscles absolutely made him a walking and talking God. Shawn could not believe that he was actually the center of attention for these two muscular, hot, hunky men. He wondered so quickly why they even had any interest in playing with him, when they obviously could just use each other and know that they were each playing with the hottest guy around. Shawn's position of being their playmate and their piece of meat for the night was way too much for him to even imagine! Shawn realized that he was in the middle of a dream experience that most, well practically all men, can only dream of ever have happening. Right now he knew that all of this wonderful experience was all due to that old broken down Chevy that just a few hours ago he wanted to get rid of so fast. Now he was becoming very convinced that he would never be able to get rid of that car. He was deciding that he would need to always keep it as his symbol of this great three-way with the two hottest built men that he had ever seen, let alone been able to touch and feel, and to have been so roughly sexually used and abused by. He had become their toy, and he liked that!

"God I don't know Bill!" Greg said. "Bill, I know I don't have the thinnest dick around, and man, putting that thing up against Shawn Boy's fat dick, —that is one hell of a thick piece of meat for you to try and get up in your ass! Bill, that's gonna be like putting an almost full sized grapefruit up in there man!"

"I know Greg! Yeah, I know! But that's what is getting me so damn hot about it! I haven't had the chance to get two dicks together that make up that much meat to try and get up in my ass for a hell of a long time, and I sure as hell don't want to pass up this opportunity now! Greg you know me well enough to know that when I get hot over something or some idea, I've gotta try it to just make sure I can do it! You guys about ready for me to force your dicks up in my ass? I may have to really force it, but men, I'm gonna know if I can take both of your dicks up in me, all at the same time, before this is over! I need those dicks up in me and right now I need 'em bad! I'm hot for this men! My ass is begging for it, guys! I want my ass filled full, real full!"

"Yeah, I think we're ready. Shawn, you ready to help me get our dicks up into Bill's ass?"

"Yeah, I'm ready, but since I've never done this, I'm not too sure of what I'm supposed to do."

"Hey Boy, just lay there and let that big thick dick of yours aim up toward the sky, and I'll put mine up against it, and when Bill squats down on it, I'll aim both of 'em for his ass. As soon as he knows they're lined up right, he's going to sit down on top of both of 'em so that he takes both of 'em up in him together. Or so he hopes anyway! He's gonna need to really spread his ass to do it, but he really wants to! Ready?"

"Yeah, I've never done this nor seen it but I sure as hell do have to admit that it is one hot action to be part of. I like this! This is really hot man, really hot!"

Bill positioned himself above the two dicks, Greg aimed them together for Bill's asshole and then said, "Sit man, sit!"

As Bill squatted down quit quickly, he steadied himself so that he didn't tip sideways, and as he drove both of the dicks up into his ass, he threw his head up toward the ceiling and let out a low, long scream.

"Oh God, —ohhhh shit man! Oh God Greg, —I've got both of you guys up in me! You're in me, —you're in me! Oh shit man that feels so fucking damn good! Oh God man! Oh, I'm so fucking glad we're doing this! Oh Greg I'm so glad you called me today and told me you and some guy were gonna be playing around together! Oh shit man, this is great! Oh man, —God my ass feels so fucking damn full! Oh Greg, his dick's as fat as a beer can isn't it? Oh God, right now I feel like I've got the whole damn case of beer up in my ass! Oh shit man! Oh God this is so fucking tight! Oh man —oh this is great! Hey guys, I'm going to fuck myself by jerking and jumping up and down on your dicks, OK?"

"Yeah enjoy yourself!" Greg said. "Boy and I are just laying here using your asshole for our fun too, so you just play anyway on our dicks all that you want to. Hey, boy, how you doing over there? You like the feel of your dick right up there hugging mine tight while we double fuck Bill's ass? You like this?"

Shawn was so overtaken by the strong feel of pressure on his dick, up inside of Bill's ass and at the same time squeezed up so tight to Greg's big dick, that he had trouble attempting a reply.

"Oh my God yes I like this! Oh Sir, I am so damn glad right now that my damn car broke down! Oh Sir, I like this. I want you guys to use me and teach me more stuff like this if you will. I've never had this much fun before. Oh Sir, when I heard those chains I was really getting kind of worried about if I should be here doing this, but oh man, — Oh God am I glad I am! Hey sir, can maybe I try to get double fucked by you two like Bill is getting from us? I never even thought about trying to get two dicks up in my ass all at once, but now that I see it, I really do want to see if I can do that! Can I try? Oh man, I'd love to know that I've got both of you guys up in me at the same time!"

"Hell yes you can, —shit yes! Hell boy, whatever you wanna try, we're game! Bill and I love to break in the new guys to some of the other kind of stuff. If you're up for it, hell yeah, we'll do it for you! Won't we Bill? Hey Bill, you in there man?"

"Oh shit yes I am. Yeah, I'm here, but just let me enjoy this for a minute or two. Oh Greg, you have got to get double fucked sometime man! Oh Greg you don't know how damn great this feels with two big thick dicks up in your ass at the same time! Hey man, let's you and me double fuck the boy, then you let him and me double fuck you, OK?"

"Shit no, man! Hell no! You know how fucking thick this guy's dick is! You think I am going to try and put it and your dick up in my ass at the same time? Are you crazy as hell or what? Fuck! I have trouble just getting your dick up in me, let alone your dick and some fucking, fence post sized, dick too! Hell no!"

"Oh Greg, loosen up!" Bill replied. "Go for the gusto man! Greg if it didn't feel so damn good, why in the hell would I keep wanting it? Greg, I've seen some pretty good sized things go up in there before. Our two dicks aren't going to rip you all apart back there! Shit man, it will put one fucking big smile on your face!"

"I don't know Bill, I don't know. Those two dicks up in my ass all at once, I don't know! I've tried it once but they sure were a hell of a lot smaller dicks than yours and his! God man, you two have big fat thick dicks!"

"Hey Greg, tell you what. Your Boy Shawn there admits that he hardly ever gets fucked! If he can take you and me, both up in his ass together at the same time, and not pull off of us right away, —then you try and take him and me. OK? Your ass sure is used to a lot more action than his is. And if his little virgin ass can take both of ours, then I think your ass should be able to take his and mine. What do you say?"

"Oh God Bill. You're making me look like some kind of a little wimp here in front of the boy! God, how in the hell can I save face unless I agree to do it! I'm telling you though, as thick as his dick is, —I'll try, —but I can't promise anything! OK?"

"Hey man, a try is all we can ask for! Deal?!"

As Bill stated "Deal" he pulled up and released Greg and Shawn's dicks from in his ass and he then climbed off of the bed, and just kind of lovingly reached around to his ass and lightly rubbed it. "Oh my butt feels so damn good men! Thanks for fucking it that way! God it feels really good now!"

"Hey man, turn around and bend over. I wanna see how open your hole is!" Greg instructed, as Bill got up from the bed.

As Bill squared his ass with Greg and Shawn, he bet over and Greg exclaimed. "Oh my God man! Look at that big hole! Bill your asshole is standing wide open! Bill I could put the blunt end of a baseball bat up in there right now and you would never know it. Squeeze your ass and see if it goes closed any."

Bill did as suggested by Greg, and his ass did close, almost completely, but not totally.

"Wow! I've never seen some guy's ass that open before!" Shawn said. "When I fuck Roger, his ass never gets that far open, and even then I guess I've never told him to bend over and let me look at it! Shit man, that is hot! Sir, you have a pretty ass! I've never seen that far up inside of a guy's ass before. Wow man, that is hot!"

Greg looked at Shawn, grinned, and said, "Hey Boy. Look good, cause right now you are looking up into the ass of another Highway Patrolman. I hadn't told you yet, but Bill here is another one of the highway's best. You've got two of the state's best playing with you tonight, so if you've never had the chance to look up in the ass of some officer, now's your chance. Bill, bend over there and let our boy see as far up inside of you and that ass of yours as he can!"

Bill did as Greg had suggested, and as he bent over he also took a butt cheek in each hand and pulled his ass open wider. As he did, he said, "It's a cops ass Boy, you're looking up in a cop's ass! Bet you've never had that chance before have you?"

Almost as weak as his voice could go, Shawn licked his lips some, and finally answered, "Hell no! I've never even thought that I'd ever get a chance to. Oh man, that is hot, that is hot! Oh shit man, I love that! Oh man, I can't believe this! I can't!"

And just as Shawn reached out with his left hand so that he could slide his finger around the inside edge of Bill's opened ass, he was stroking his own dick with his right hand, and he added, "Oh gawd. Every time I see some officer now, I'm always gonna wonder if his ass looks just like yours does, and I know damn well, I'm always gonna wanna tell him to drop his pants and let me see his ass and then reach out and spread it wide open like this! Oh men, this is so fucking hot to me! This is hot! I can not believe that I sitting here looking up in the ass of a hot highway patrolman!"

Bill then suggested that Greg get rid of the chaps since he was probably going to have to take them off anyway, when his turn comes to getting double fucked, and Bill then reached over and grabbed some more Crisco and told Shawn to bend over the bed for a minute. As Shawn did, Bill packed his ass with a good supply of grease and after wiping his hands off, he laid down on the bed and pushed his crotch up against Greg's so that their two hard-ons were standing up, right side by side.

"OK Boy, climb up here and get ready to squat down on us. You're gonna take two highway patrolmen up in your ass all at the same time! Yeah, —that's right! OK Boy, whenever you are ready, just start squatting and I'll aim our dicks for your little asshole. You sit down on us as fast or as slowly as you want. OK?"

"Oh God yeah!" Shawn answered. "God, I've got to admit that I never ever thought of the idea of trying to get two cocks up in my ass at the same time, and I will admit that although I'm about as excited about trying this as anything I've ever done, I'm kind of nervous and hope like hell I can do it! Oh shit man, this is gonna feel like I'm trying to put something like a watermelon up in me! Oh man, I hope I can do this!"

Then looking at Bill, Shawn asked. "I've got to do this or Sir doesn't have to do it, does he? I've got to get you guys up in me, don't I?"

"Yeah man! Yeah! You've got to take both of us so that Greg has to do it. He agreed that if you can do it, then he'll try, so do your damn best Boy, take us! You'll do it, you've gotta do it!" Bill encouraged. "Hey Boy, you've got to do it since I made that deal with your Sir man! You fuck yourself with our dicks and then he has to do it too! So show me how much you like two dicks up in there all at once man! Fuck yourself! Sit down on those dicks and put 'em up in you! Do something for yourself that you have never done before! Use our cocks, man! Double fuck yourself!"

Shawn took a deep breath, and then moving just so slightly so that it did feel like the tip of Bill and Greg's dicks were aimed right at the asshole spot, he suddenly let his legs fly out from under himself and he immediately impaled himself on both of the dicks and let out a scream of,—"Oh Shit!!!!! Oh God man!! Oh crap!!!!!!!!" He actually reached up and wiped a tear from his cheek that had slipped out as he accepted the sharp pain in his ass and then in a little calmer tone, he realize how loud he had been and after laughing a little he added, "Oh God guys! I hope nobody was outside when I yelled! Oh shit man, I didn't expect it to feel that way at all. Oh God man, it feels so damn good! God I hope nobody heard me scream! Oh guys, let me fuck myself on you for a minute, OK?"

"Hell yes, it's OK!" Bill said. "That's why you're using us man! Jump up and down on 'em! Let yourself feel us up in there! Yeah—fuck yourself with these two dicks! Like it, don't you? You really like that much stuck up in there, don't you? Feels good don't it? Like it, don't you?"

"Oh hell yes I do! Oh Sir— please let us do this to you! Oh you will like it! Oh God it feels so damn good! Oh wow! God men, —maybe I really do like having some big stuff rammed up in my ass. Shit men, —I never knew until now that I liked this kind of playing around! Hell men, I think maybe you two have taught the new kid some fun stuff tonight! Oh God man this is so good! Oh man I like this! Oh men I don't want this to stop! Oh men, I like having your dicks up in my ass! Oh don't make me get off of 'em! Oh let me ride 'em some more! Oh every time I see an officer I'm gonna wish he was up in my ass like this! Oh yeah!"

"Well don't act like the night is over yet Boy! It's hardly even started, especially if you know you like some of this kind of playing." Greg replied. "Bill and I have all night if we need it, and if you want it, so don't sound like the night is over yet. OK?"

"Well, —yeah." Shawn answered. "I didn't mean to sound like it was all over, I guess I was just trying to say thanks for what you guys are showing me! Damn, I like this! I guess my sex life has been a little too tame and calm for what I do like! Those chains kind of scared the hell out of me when I first heard them, but now I think they sound like bells. When you first chained me down, I was really wondering if I was out of my mind, but now, —hey —what can I say? I guess when you totally trust some guy, and you like to be dominated and completely controlled, then maybe the terror is part of the fun?

Is that right guys? I mean, Sir—and you too Sir, since I'm not sure what I'm supposed to call you!"

"Hey Boy, you call your main man, 'Sir', and you call me 'Daddy'. OK? You are Boy, Greg is Sir and I am Daddy! OK?"

"Yeah, I like that! Sir and Daddy! Oh man, I do like that! That really gives me the feeling that whatever you two men say, I have to obey! Right? Is that kind of right?"

"Yes, you are completely right!" Bill replied. "So I take it that you are now pretty well turning yourself over to your Sir and your Daddy, and we can pretty well play and do as we want with you for the rest of the night. Right?"

"Oh God is that what I said? Oh shit! Huuhhhh—well I guess so. Oh shit man, what am I saying? Yeah—I guess so. Hey —to admit that, —to be willing to just turn myself and my body over to two guys that look, and are built like you two big hunky muscled guys, is pretty scary, but at the same time, so damn exciting that I would be pissed at myself forever, if I didn't do it! Yeah—I admit that I might be out of my mind, but I know that if I said 'No', I would kick myself for the rest of my life that I didn't take the one chance that I had, to let you two hot muscular macho studly guys just take me and use me however you wanted. Oh God man, I hope I'm not out of my mind!"

"No boy, you're not out of your mind!" Greg reassured him. "You might wonder a little later if you're up to everything that we want to do with you, but do trust us, no bodily harm will happen to you. We just are not in to physical harm. Now maybe some temporary pain, but nothing that is going to harm you, OK? Hey guy, whatever fun we have with you is making fun for us too! This is for all of us to really have some good fun with each other, and use each other every way we can! OK?"

"Yes Sir—I guess so! I know I'm too damn excited and turned on by what has happened so far, — that I know I wouldn't be able to live with myself if I turned this down. Yeah, —just don't do anything like cut me or anything like that! OK? Please? I've just never gotten to play this way with two guys like you two, or like this!"

"No problem Boy, no problem! Just fun! It's all just for fun. Your Sir man and I don't find good willing play stuff like you very often, so we sure are going to have our fun with you, put we sure are going to protect you too, —since maybe we can get together and do this again sometime. OK? Understand?"

"Yeah, —yeah, —I do, Daddy, I do! I appreciate you telling me that I'm safe. I appreciate that! I like being kind of used by two guys like you two, I just want to know I won't end up in a hospital or something!"

Shawn double fucked his ass for quite a pit of time, and he kept telling his Daddy and Sir of how damn excited this night was turning out to be and how excited he was about knowing that he had both of their dicks up in his ass at the same time. After an extensive fucking, he finally admitted that maybe it was time for him to stop all of the jumping up and down on the dicks, and that he wanted to get started doing the double fucking of Sir, that Sir had agreed to, if he took both of the other guys' dicks.

"OK Boy, lay down on that bed and get that big fat dick of yours up in the air." Bill said. "Greg, did you get your ass all greased up? Boy has got one big fat dick that he wants to put up in your ass, and then after he's up in you, then I'm gonna come up in beside him, OK?"

"Yeah I guess!" Greg answered. "Got to admit that getting that fat dick and then yours to all up in my ass all at once, is still a fucking concern to me! I'm not so sure I can do this!"

"Hell yes Greg, you can do this! I've seen bigger things than his dick and my dick go up in there. Greg, I've had my hand up in there before! You've just got some mental hang-ups and as soon as you have both of us up in there, you're gonna be so damn glad you did! Now squat down on him, and after he's up in there, then I'm gonna be coming up, in beside him."

Greg started to squat down onto Boy's dick and as he did, he said, "Oh my God man he has got one hell of a fat dick! My God Bill, I've never had a dick this thick up in my ass before! Man my ass feels full already! Shit man he is thick! My gawd man, he got a big dick on him!"

Bill watched as Greg impaled himself down onto Shawn's wide dick, and when he was quite sure Shawn was well up and into Greg's ass, he pointed his own dick right at Greg's asshole and by thrusting his midsection up, he pushed the tip end of it up and into Greg's ass.

"Oh shit man! Oh, God man!" Greg yelled out almost as loud as Boy had done earlier. "Oh God Bill, —oh shit man! Oh God Bill! If you are going to put that up in me, push it up in all of the way right away, —right now! God Bill get it up in me! Yeah, —push it up in me! Oh man that hurts, but get it up in me as far as it will go right away! Let me know I've got everything up in there so I can try and get used to it! Oh God man my ass is so fucking full! Oh shit man, —my ass is tight! Oh Bill push up in me! Are you all the way in? Oh God my ass feels stretched."

"Yeah Greg, I'm in all the way! You've got me and Boy all the way up in you now. Relax and just let your ass get used to it. Give it just a minute and you are going to be ready to fuck yourself with our dicks up in you! In a minute you'll wanna give us both a kiss since we made you sit on us. How you feeling? Getting used to 'em yet?"

"Oh I guess so! When you first pushed up into me it really hurt for a second and then it quit, and then when you pushed in again, it hurt again. That's why I told you to go all the way so that I would know it was all over and then I could try to relax my ass. Yeah, now it's feeling pretty good. Yeah, I have to admit, it feels damn full, but it's feeling pretty good now! Kind of feels like getting fisted some doesn't it? Kind of, —just kind of doesn't it?"

"Well, Greg my dear man. I don't know, because you're the one that's been fisted before, not me, —but to me I'd think getting fisted is a hell of a lot more forceful and painful back there than getting a couple of dicks up my ass, even when one of them is as fat as Boy toy's here!"

"Do you guys do fisting!" Shawn all of a sudden asked as he heard Greg mention it. "Oh God you guys aren't planning on fisting me tonight are you? Oh hell I never thought about something like that! Please tell me you guys are not planning on trying to fist me! Please!"

"Hey I'm not promising anything!" Bill replied. "You turned yourself over to us for the rest of the night a little while ago, and I don't remember making a list of what we would or would not do! Remember you already told us that when you first heard the chains, that scared the hell out of you but then you found out that everything was OK. So, maybe, just maybe getting some hand up in your tight little ass might not be such a bad thing either! And beside, maybe it's not our hand up in your ass, maybe it's your hand up in one of our asses! See, there are two ways to everything, right?"

"Yeah, right! Yeah, OK. But please, I really don't think I could take something that big up in my ass. I know that has to hurt. God Bill, do you really have guys put their hands up in your ass? Do you really do that? Oh God man! Oh God that sounds hot, but shit man, that has got to hurt! That's really letting another man take complete control over you isn't it? Oh God, I like the idea of that, some guy taking complete control over me, but shit man,— God, that's putting a lot up in some guy's ass. Oh fuck man! That sounds so damn hot to me! Oh shit man, I'd like to see that happen. Maybe one of you guys will do that to the other one and I can watch it happen? I'd like to see it!"

"Hey boy, don't go getting all confused here. It's your Daddy man that takes a hand up in his ass. I've put my hand up in his ass before, but I've never had it done to me."

As Bill and Shawn talked about the fisting and Shawn's pleading to not be fisted, although he did admit that he sure would like to see it done to somebody else, Greg had been enjoying his position of sitting on their stiff cocks. He was definitely finding out that getting double fucked by two big dicks was a pretty good experience. He was enjoying having his ass packed full, he was fucking himself by bouncing up and down so that both of the dicks would go up into him as far as possible, they just almost come completely out before he sat back down on them again and rammed them back up inside again.

Bill was laying in the position to where he could see Greg's face, and as Greg made wild passionate sex with himself by fucking himself, using the two dicks that were stuck up into his ass, Bill grinned at him, and Greg grinned back, expressing his complete approval and enjoyment of having their dicks pushed up in his butt and his ability to do some wild, self fucking, by jumping up and down on 'em. Bill knew that Greg was now very glad that Bill had rather forced him into getting the double fuck!

Greg finally slowed down some from his sitting and bouncing up and down on the two dicks, and as he looked at Bill he said, "Hey you know what man,— I've got some stuff in the back of the truck in my tool box that I think maybe we need to get and use on the Boy! What do you think?"

Bill grinned a broad grin and replied, "Yeah, if you're talking about what I think you are! Yeah, let's do."

CHAPTER FOUR:

Toys in the Tool Box

Greg immediately pulled up and off of the two dicks and as Bill and Shawn untangled their legs, Shawn asked. "Hey what kind of things is Sir talking about being in his tool box? Daddy, what's he talking about?"

Bill looked at Shawn and just replied, "Hang tight man, hang tight! You'll see!"

Greg looked at Bill and said, "Hey man, I just realized I don't have any pants to put on in here. Will you throw your pants on and go get that box that's hidden in the bottom of the tool box? Here's the key, and down in the bottom is a cardboard box that is sealed closed with some shipping tape. Bring that box in here. OK?"

Bill grabbed his pants, put them on and headed out to the truck. Greg's Dodge Ram had a large truck bed tool box in it and Bill got it unlocked, and found the cardboard box that Greg had asked him to go find!"

As Bill returned back into the motel room, he quickly realized that Greg was using some of this rather "down time" to do some of his own "down time," —down in front of Shawn's thick rod. Greg was fucking his own mouth now, with the same thick dick that he had, just a few minutes ago, been fucking his ass with. He was very active in pushing and pulling Shawn's body up to and then away from his face so that he could fuck his own mouth with Shawn's rod.

"Oh man!" Bill said as he saw the action happening in the motel room. "Hey, taking a pretty big full, mouth full, there aren't you buddy? Felt so damn good up in your ass, decided you needed it down your throat too uh? Yeah man—fuck your face, man!"

Greg glanced over toward Bill and kind of just shook his head "Yes," to let him know he had heard the comment.

Shawn had kind of lost his intimidation of playing with these two hot hunky very well built guys. Two guys that also happened to be somewhat older than he was, which made the calling them "Daddy" and "Sir" a little easier to do, and when Greg got down on his knees and put Shawn's hard-on into his mouth, Shawn then realized that he sure had something to offer this party, something that he now knew they both wanted, and he started fucking Greg's mouth like he knew he was one of the main players! Shawn had a firm solid grip on Greg's head, and he was taking a very big advantage of Greg's hunger for feeling that big fat dick in his mouth. He knew Greg was fucking his own mouth with his dick, and Shawn was helping him fuck it as hard as he wanted.

Bill stripped off the shorts that he had on to go get the box from the bed of the truck, and after he laid the box on the bed, he ripped the packaging tape from it and opened it up to see just what kinds of good toys his buddy Greg was keeping hidden in his truck tool box.

After pulling out a couple of different sized butt plugs, some leather cock straps, some clips and also some candles, Bill removed a couple of towels that were in the box and then exclaimed, "Holy shit! Holy shit man! Greg who in the hell takes this damn thing up in his ass?" Bill was holding up an 18 inch long, double headed dildo that was about an inch in diameter. Then as he pulled yet another dildo out of the box, he actually let out another rather loud, "Holly shit man! Oh my gawd! Holly crap man! Who in the hell can take this damn thing?"

The additional dildo that Bill was examining was a very, very thick dildo that was two inches in diameter and had a 13 inch long shaft on it, above its very hefty set of balls.

Greg looked over enough to watch Bill hold both of the long dildos up in the air and rather examine them, and as he pulled off of Shawn's dick he replied, "Hey Bill, those are my buddies! Those guys and I have gotten to be very close! I told you a few weeks ago that I had found some good stuff to use, and now you can see what I was talking about! Don't knock 'em till you try 'em, man!"

"Shit man, you think I'm going to be trying one of these? I might get probably about the first four or five inches of this thinner one up in me, but shit man, —this thick one is a fucking monster dick!"

Shawn looked over to see the items that Bill was expounding on about, but he said nothing.

Greg then looked up at Shawn from his kneeling position in front of Shawn's rod, and asked, "Well Boy, you sure are pretty quiet. You like what you're looking at there?"

Shawn did not immediately answer Greg, but Greg did notice somewhat of an admiring smile appear on Shawn's face.

"So Boy, talk to me! You like what Bill is holding over there? You smile much more and I'm going to know for damn sure that you're starting to wish one of them was up inside of you, aren't you?"

"Oh Sir." Shawn answered. "Sir, I've seen dildos like those advertised in some mags before, but I've never really seen one for real, and yeah, I will admit that whenever I've seen one of them in a picture, I always kind of wondered just what it would feel like to try and get one up in my ass. Shit man! That is one hell of a lot of stuff to be sticking up in your butt, but like I did say, those ads sure do make a guy kind of wonder."

Greg turned to Bill and said, "Hey guy, I think we have ourselves a Ginny pig here! Hear what the boy just said? Hell man, I think his ass is hungry for one of those dildos!"

"Right Boy?" Greg asked as he looked back toward Shawn.

"Sir, —yeah, —yeah, — I guess. I guess I've already admitted that they look exciting to me. I don't think I can get either one of them up in my ass, but yeah, —yeah, I've always wondered what it would feel like if you can do it."

"Greg, how much of these do you get up in your ass, man!" Bill asked with deep concern. "Greg, can you take all of these? Do you take the whole damn thing?"

"I can take the whole thing of the thinner one. I've taken it up in my ass the whole way two or three times now, and the fatter one, I can take half of the length, and am still trying to take the whole thing. Like I said Bill, don't knock 'em until you try 'em! I was just like Boy here. I had seen 'em in some mags and they got me kind of all excited, so when I saw 'em in a book store, I decided I was game, and I'm not sorry I got 'em. They feel damn good once you've got 'em up in you!"

"So shit man! You gonna show the Boy and me how you take 'em? I mean, if you can take that damn much up in your ass, I wanna watch that!"

"I do too!" Shawn rather meekly added. "Sir, can we watch you put those up in your ass, Sir? Please, I wanna watch that!"

"OK guys, let me lay down here on the bed, and hand me the Crisco. I need to get it all greased up and get some grease up in my ass too. I'll use the skinnier one. That's the one I can get all the way up in me. But, got to tell you guys right now, it takes time. Don't expect me to just slam this whole damn think up in me all at once. It takes time to get stuff all opened up and lined up in there so I can slide it up in me. OK?"

As Bill was standing beside the bed, watching his Buddy Greg grease up the entire length of the dildo, he was unconsciously stroking his own rod of meat, as was Shawn. The idea that they were going to be watching this hunk of a hot muscular guy put 18 inches of a dildo up in his ass was getting both of them turned on.

Greg laid back on the bed and put his legs up in the air so that his ass was completely exposed and ready for the entry of 18 inches of dick. Fake dick, —true, but nobody really cared if it was a real dick or a dildo dick. Bill and Shawn positioned themselves so that they each had a very clear and open line of sight at Greg's ass.

Greg positioned the tip of the dildo right at his ass. Slowly he pulled the dildo in toward his ass and let the tip of it slide in. Slowly he continued to pull more and more of it up toward himself, and slowly Bill and Shawn watched as inch by inch, slowly the dildo disappeared up in Greg's ass.

As the first half of the 18 inches disappeared and was no longer visible, Bill just simply let out a simple, "Shit man! I can not believe this." He then looked at Shawn to see what his reaction was, and he realized that Shawn was completely taken in with what he was watching, and what was happening.

"God Greg, doesn't that hurt?" Bill asked.

Calmly and almost totally quietly Greg replied, "No. No it feels good! Just gotta take it slow and let everything get all ready for it, and then just let it go up in you! It's different, but man, it feels good!"

As Greg was talking, he continued to slide more and more of the entire 18 inches up into himself, and suddenly Bill and Shawn realized that Greg now had everything except for about two inches of the entire 18 inches of dildo, up in his ass.

"Oh my God!" Bill stated, and not calmly. "My God Greg, you've got almost the whole damn thing up in you! Shit man! You're not gonna put the rest of it up in you are you? For God sake Greg, —don't push anymore of it up in you! You'll loose it Greg!"

"Hey calm down Bill." Greg answered. "I can put the whole damn thing up in me. It's not gonna get lost. I've put the end of it up in me each time that I've put all of if up in me. I can put it up in there and as long as I just lay here and relax, it'll stay put, but if I move any, then it starts coming out like a big line of shit. It's not gonna stay up in there. It feels good, and maybe part of it's just the fun, that I've done something crazy like that to my ass, but it keeps trying to slide back out!"

As Greg looked at Bill, he added, "You know Bud. I told you once how I get these real weird feelings once in awhile that I kind of want to do crazy unexplained things to myself that I really can't explain, and really can't mention to anybody else or they'd have me committed. I didn't tell you at the time, but, well this is one of 'em. Taking a hand up in me as far as possible is another one. I know it's weird stuff to do to myself, or to have done to me, but for some reason it's a mental high for me to do it. I think I kind of need to prove to myself that I can take the rough and rugged stuff, once in awhile. You know, when I was a kid, before I got all beefed up, I got a lot of teasing for being the small guy, and I guess now I need to prove to myself that I can take the rougher stuff. Better than taking drugs, I guess!"

"Hell yeah, I agree with that one!" Bill answered.

"OK, so now, —do the Boy and I get to watch that whole thing come back out of your ass, or what do you do now?"

"Yeah. Just sit tight guys. I've got 18 inches of dildo wanting to get out of me, so just sit tight."

Greg then rather propped his feet up, and with a very slight squeeze of his gut, he started the end of the dildo out of his ass. Inch by inch, all 18 inches of the dildo slid out and finally fell onto the bed.

"Oh shit man!" Bill exclaimed. "Shit man, I have never in my entire life watched anything like that! Greg, I can not believe it! You had an entire 18 inches of dildo stuck up in there! God Greg, how you feel? You OK?"

"Oh yeah, I'm OK. I'm OK, but letting that slide out just makes me horny for that thicker one. Bill, —wanna slide part of that one up in me?"

"Oh shit Greg, are you serious? You want me to fuck your ass with that damn big thing?"

"Yeah! Yeah, I do, or I wouldn't have suggested it to you. Now I can't take all of it like the skinny one, but I can take most of it. Wanna try it on me?"

"Hell yes I do man! Shit yes!"

Bill handed the skinnier dildo to Shawn to get it out of the way, and he then greased up the thicker dildo and got it ready to go up into Greg's ass.

Bill got Greg is position and slowly aimed the tip of the fatter dildo at Greg's asshole.

"Now Bill, this one is a hell of a lot thicker to my ass than that other one is, so this one has to go in real slow! I've got to get my ass opened up for this one. I've gotta get it opened up some if I'm gonna take this one. I've never had another guy put it up in me before. I've always done it myself, so we might need to figure out just how to do it. Since I can just lay down flat, and don't have to reach down there to handle it, it might be easier for me to take it this time. Just take it slow. OK?"

"Yeah, OK! Yeah, you just tell me what to do, OK?"

"OK, just start it up in me like it was a real dick, and if you hit a wrong spot or go too fast, I'll let you know."

As Shawn came back in the room, with the dildo in his hand, from the bathroom, he stood there for a moment and watched Bill start the dildo up into Greg's ass. He then asked, "Hey Sir. Would it be OK if I tried to take some of this one up in my ass while Daddy man does your ass? I'd kind of like to see if I can take part of this one."

"Yeah, of course Boy! Get some grease on it and put some on your ass and lay down here beside me. Yeah, I wanna see how much of that your ass can eat too! Here lay down here Boy! Put it in you!"

Shawn got the can of Crisco and greased not only the dildo but his ass as well. He laid down beside Greg, and followed Greg's earlier example of how to get the dildo started up into his ass, and then keep sliding it in, inch by inch.

Shawn was now dildo fucking himself, and Bill was dildo fucking Greg.

"God this is hot action, man!" Greg said to nobody in particular. Shit men, this looks like a scene out of some gay porno video. I like this! I sure as hell did not think my day would end up anything like this! Boy, I am damn glad your car broke down today, and Bill I'm fucking glad your old lady is out of town tonight so that you could join us here! Things are working out pretty damn good, I'd say!"

Slowly Bill managed to work a little more of the two inch thick dildo up into Greg's ass, and as he was doing that, he would occasionally look over to see how Shawn was doing on his own, self fucking actions. He smiled more than once in appreciation of how quickly Shawn was managing to eat more and more of that 18 inches of 'dick'.

"Shit Boy!" Bill expounded in amazement. "Shit man, do you realize that you damn near have that whole 18 inches up in you? Do you know how much of that thing you have taken up in your ass?"

Shawn tried to look down toward his ass a little, and then said, "I thought I was getting most of it up in me, but I couldn't tell for sure. How much more have I got to go, Daddy?"

"Only about four more inches, man!" Bill replied. "Shit man for being a guy that supposedly never gets fucked, you sure as hell have got one hot and hungry asshole."

"My God Greg! Your Boy has got nearly that whole damn thing up in his ass! Shit man, —for somebody that hardly ever gets played with back there, he sure as hell has got one hungry ass! Greg, your Boy is just about to outdo you in the fucking business, unless we can manage to get this whole thing up in you so that you're still one step ahead of him."

"Hey Bill, when he got double fucked by us, I figured then, that he was a real player and had an ass that was anxious for a hell of a lot more than it was getting! That's why I decided to get this box out of the truck. I figured he'd like 'em, and I wanted to see just how much of 'em he was willing to try and take."

"Well he sure as the hell is going for that one for sure! I've played around with my ass for years now, and I've never taken 18 inches of dick or anything else up in my ass!"

Then looking at Shawn, Bill asked, "Boy, buddy. You've really never had something like that up in your ass before, right?"

"No. No I never have, but I will admit that if anybody that I had ever played with before had told me they had one like this available, I would've begged to use it. Every time I've seen one pictured, I've wanted to try it. I just never had a good opportunity to buy one or try one. Man I'm glad I get to use this one! I like it! It feels good! Hey, Daddy, it feels like there's only about maybe and inch or two to go before I have all of it up in my ass, right?"

Bill looked over to check out the situation and he said, "Shit yes man! You have just about the whole damn thing up in you. It looks like only about one inch of dildo sticking out."

Shawn turned toward Greg and asked. "OK Sir! Got a question! If I can take the end of this and push it up inside of me, it's OK to do that? I mean, it will come back out OK when I want it to, right?"

"Yeah Boy! It'll come back out! If you want to, put your finger on the tip of it, and push it up in. You'll feel it slide up in you, and all of sudden your asshole will slam shut on your finger. You'll know you are then, laying there with 18 inches of dick stuffed up in your ass! Going to do it?"

"Yeah, yeah!" Shawn answered. "I got all hot and excited when I saw you do it, and so yeah, I want to do it! Yeah, here goes! Oh yeah, —hey, —hey man, —it's all up in me! Hey guys, I've got the whole damn thing up in me! Oh shit! Oh hell, —I never thought I'd be putting an 18 inch dildo up in my ass today! Oh God! Oh shit man! Oh man, I like this! Hey Sir! I want to call Roger and tell him. Hey, can I do that?"

"Hell yeah if you want to and you don't think he'll get pissed. Just don't make your man mad about anything. OK?"

"Yeah, OK! No, I won't make him mad! Probably a little jealous of what I'm getting to do, but no, he won't get mad. He'll probably wish he was here and doing this stuff too!"

Shawn dialed.

"Hey Rog Honey! Yeah, —hey Hon, you will never believe what in the hell is happening. No, no, —no, I'm OK, —I'm alright! Hon, I am more than alright! Believe me man, I am! Hon, I am having the time of my life! Guess what in the hell I have up in my ass! Yeah, an entire 18 inch long dildo! Yeah, —Greg had it in his truck and he put it up in himself first, and now Bill is running another fatter one up in him, and I'm using the skinny one on myself. Oh Hon, it feels so damn good! Yeah my ass is closed around the end of it! Yeah, completely! Yeah—the whole damn thing! No—Greg told me before I pushed it up in there that it'll try and come back out all by itself, and it is! I have to keep squeezing my asshole shut to keep it in. No —yeah —no it feels so good! Hey Hon, we have got to buy some dildos like these! Yeah, the one Bill is using on Greg right now is —oh yeah, Greg said it's two inches thick. Do you realize how thick two inches is when it's going up in a guy's ass? Hey man, it looks good going up in Greg's ass, but I'm in the wrong place to really watch it. Yeah, —I will. I'll fill you in more tomorrow! But Honey, I really do want us to buy some dildos like these. I just found out that I like having a big 18 inch dick up in my ass! Yeah, —I know it's not real, but shit man, —it still feels good! OK, —yeah, —I'll talk to you tomorrow if not more tonight, OK? Yeah love you Hon, bye, —bye!"

Shawn hung up the phone and told the other two men, "I think Roger is glad I'm getting it up in the ass. He sounded excited that I'm getting into some hot ass play. Maybe I've been too standoffish to tell him that I want my ass played with more often. Hey, guys. Maybe this will help Roger and me get into some new stuff that'll be good for us! Yeah, —I do know one thing, we'll be buying some big dildos as soon as we can."

Bill continued to work on Greg and on Greg's ass with the thicker dildo.

"Hey man, got to tell you if you are not already aware, your Boy has taken the whole 18 inches. Unless you are gonna act like some kind of a wimp, you better take the rest of this dick, man. You willing to try?"

"Yeah Bill, yeah. Since you're putting it up in me and I can just lay here and relax, maybe I can take all of it. Yeah man, yeah—I wanna know I can take the whole damn thing. Just go slow and careful. I don't really want to rip my insides all up! OK?"

Shawn continued to play with himself and let the 18 incher slide out just slightly so that he could handle it and playfully fuck himself with it. He truly enjoyed the feeling of the long dildo going in and out of his ass. The more excited he got about the great feeling, the faster he worked on himself.

Bill found it quite amusing and interesting that Shawn was into fucking himself with that dildo as fast and as roughly as he was doing. He knew most guys that use a dildo on themselves usually take it pretty slowly and calmly. Shawn was not taking anything slowly or calmly!

"Easy man, easy man!" Bill suggested to Shawn. "Don't rip yourself all up in there. Enjoy that thing, just don't tear stuff up!"

Shawn looked over at Bill, grinned and then answered with a, "Thanks! I guess I was getting kind of wild with it wasn't I? I've seen these pictured before, like I said, but I've never had one up in my ass before, and guys, I've got to tell you, I like it! Damn I like it!"

"I can see that!" Bill answered back. "I can see you and your ole asshole are really living it up! Just kind of slow down on yourself for a little while, and let me finish up here with Greg and then we'll use this one on you. I'm not even asking if you want to, because the way you are fucking yourself with that one, I know damn well you want this one too, don't you?"

"Yeah, —yeah I do admit it! This one is sure fun, but yet I gotta admit that I want to see how much of that one I can take. It looks so damn fat and thick just going up in Greg's ass. He's taking it though isn't he? His ass is eating that thing, isn't it?"

"Yeah, he's letting this thing get up in there like it belongs up in there. Look at that smile on his face! He's enjoying this one just as much as you are that one, but just a little slower and a little more calmly!"

Shawn watched Bill work on Greg's ass with the fatter dildo and then told 'em, "Hey guys, I'm really enjoying this tonight! I am so damn glad we're doing this! There is no way in hell that earlier today I thought I'd be involved in something this exciting! Oh man! I love this! I think my sex life just chanced today! You know guys, —every time I've seen a dildo pictured that was kind of like these, I just kind of closed my eyes and wondered if times like this ever happened for other guys, or was that just a big deep wish and a desire on my part. Men, there is no way that you guys will ever know how exciting this night is to me! I have wanted to be involved is some wild and kinky sex stuff with a couple of guys for years now, and until today, it just never happened. I'm living in sexual heaven right now! I've seen some gay porno movies before, and right now I feel like I'm in the middle of one of them. I like that! I want action, and I guess I want some kinky action, don't I? Yeah, when you get as much of that up in Greg as you can, then I wanna see how much of it I can take! My ass wants it! Can I lay here and let one of you guys put it up in me like you're doing to my big Sir?"

"Yeah of course you can. Look at how much of it your Sir man has up in him now."

"Oh shit man!" Shawn exclaimed as he looked over and realized that Greg had all of it except for only about the last three inches up in his ass.

Greg laid there and smiled greatly as his buddy Bill continued his adventure of putting the entire larger dildo up into his ass.

"How you doing Buddy?" Bill asked, as he gave the bottom end of the dildo one last and firm shove, in all the way up to its balls, to let Greg know that he had the entire shaft of that thick dildo up in him.

"Yeah push on it Bill, push on it! Oh man! I didn't know if I could get that whole damn thing up in me or not, but I guess I made it, right?" Greg happily asked.

"Yes you sure did Buddy!" Bill replied. "Yes you did! How you feeling? Feeling OK?"

"Yeah, I feel OK, just kid of stuffed down there! I don't feel like I can bend my body too much. That dildo's pretty stiff isn't it?"

"Yeah it is!" Bill replied. "I noticed that too. You've really got something more like part of a wooden baseball bat up in there than some dick. But then, hey, —if a real man was supporting a dick this damn big and this thick, maybe it would be this damn stiff too. I've sure never had the chance to find out about a guy hung like that, so I guess we'll just have to assume."

As Greg and Bill discussed the stiffness and the thickness of the dildo that Greg had totally up in his ass, Bill was making sure that Greg got the full effect of having his ass full by slowly pulling it back and forth as if he was getting a true fucking from the invisible man that it should be connected to it.

"How's that feeling? What does that feel like up inside? Does that feel good?"

"Oh shit yes it does!" Greg replied. "Got to admit it does feel rather different that far up inside of me, but it feels good. I know it probably sounds kind of weird, but the best feeling that I have is the feeling of accomplishment of getting it all up in me. Isn't that weird that doing that is making me happy? Is that some kind of a childhood hangover of wanting to prove to myself or somebody else, that I can do something like this?"

"No Greg, I really don't think it's weird! I think we all have our items in life that we would like to know that we can accomplish, and having half of a tree trunk rammed up in your ass is yours, I guess!" Bill replied to his Buddy as he also laughed.

"Oh shut the hell up and fuck my ass with that damn tree trunk!" Greg replied as he too laughed. "I've got all of it in me, and now I wanna feel it up in me. Fuck my ass Bill, fuck my ass!"

"Hey guys," Shawn interrupted, "Can I push on the end of that and kind of fuck Sir's ass a little before you get done?"

"Oh God yes Boy! I'm sorry! Greg and I were both so damn excited that he took the whole damn thing up in there that we kind of got all wrapped up in just what we were doing. Here, grab a hold of the balls on it and fuck the man's ass."

Shawn carefully and slowly got up on his hands and knees and positioned himself so that he could play with the dildo and also play with Greg's dick. When he did, that put his ass directly up in the air, and Bill realized that he was still holding the other dildo up in his ass.

"Oh shit man! You've still got the other one up in your ass, don't you Boy? Shit man, I'm gonna use it to fuck your ass for you, just like you were doing to yourself earlier! Get ready Boy, I'm gonna use that dildo on you!"

Shawn was playing with Greg's butt and the thick dildo ramming it up in and then back out as quickly and as forcefully as Greg would let him. He was bent over taking Greg's hardon in his mouth and sucking on it to the same rhythm that he was using on his ass with the dildo, and at the same time, Bill was actively fucking Shawn's butt with the thinner dildo, although now, since Shawn was bent over, it was not all the way up and in! Bill wasn't being exactly slow and careful with the dildo that was stuck in Shawn's ass. He had see Shawn getting pretty rough with himself when he was fucking his ass good and actively earlier, so he had decided that if he wanted to get Shawn really good and hot, then he needed to use as much activity back there as possible. And he was! Shawn's ass was getting a good fast and furious dildo fucking!

"Shit man!" Bill stated. "God Boy, you sure as hell do like it rough in your ass don't you? I swear if any guy was ramming my ass with a dildo like

I have been doing to yours, I'd be slugging him in the jaw to get him to quit. Shawn Boy, I can't believe how you have all of a sudden decided that you just can't hardly get rough enough with anything going on up in your ass! I can tell right now, you're the kind of a guy that will really get into getting fisted! You may not have had a guy's hand up in your butt yet, but I can tell that if that doesn't happen yet tonight, it sure as the hell will soon!

Your ass is almost hanging a big sign stating, — 'Fist Me, And Fist Me Deep'!"

I know it's not gonna happen tonight guys, but I will tell you both something, it is gonna happen! Roger and I are gonna get both of you guys up to our place sometime, for a full week-end of playing, and I know damn well that if I have not been back down here before then and taken a fist from one of you guys, I will that week-end! I'm not gonna get it until I know I'm getting it from one of the two hottest and sexiest, Highway Patrolmen on the roads! God! You guys are good!"

ABOUT THE AUTHOR:

Wade Wright

Wade Wright is an older gay gentleman, (using <u>his</u> wording here now) that lives in Arizona, alone, except for his puppy of about 15 years, and is semi-retired. One "normal" marriage, and two sadly shortened gay partnerships, have given Wade a perspective of living very different types of lives, and wishing some of his stories were from "true life adventures!"

APARTMENT 117

APARTMENT 117

117

a novel by

WADE WRIGHT

A
BONER
BOOK

The Two Straight Guys

a novel by

Wade Wright

A
BONER
BOOK